P____ **for A House for the Season:**

The Miser of Mayfair

Being the First Volume of
A House for the Season

M.C. Beaton

Canvas

Constable & Robinson Ltd
55–56 Russell Square
London WC1B 4HP
www.constablerobinson.com

First published in the US by St Martin's Press, 1986

This paperback edition published in the UK by Canvas,
an imprint of Constable & Robinson Ltd, 2013

A copy of the British Library Cataloguing in
Publication Data is available from the British Library

ISBN: 978-1-78033-305-2 (paperback)

Typeset by TW Typesetting, Plymouth, Devon

Printed and bound in the UK

1 3 5 7 9 10 8 6 4 2

To the Mulcare family –
Ann, Tony, Patrick and Charlotte

History is but a tiresome thing in itself; it becomes more agreeable the more romance is mixed up with it. The great enchanter has made me learn many things which I should never have dreamed of studying, if they had not come to me in the form of amusement.

Thomas Love Peacock

PROLOGUE

Mr Glowry used to say that his house was no better than a spacious kennel, for every one in it led the life of a dog.
THOMAS LOVE PEACOCK, *NIGHTMARE ABBEY*

It had been a long winter, and the spring of 1807 seemed an unconscionable time in coming. The days were blustery and cold, the skies leaden and dismal.

But in the heart of London's Mayfair there were already signs that spring was struggling through the gloom. Daffodils were blowing in the tussocky grass of Hyde Park, and a cherry tree at the corner of South Audley Street raised its weighted branches of pink blossom to the lowering sky.

Outside the town houses, from Grosvenor Square to St James's Square, brass was being energetically polished, window frames painted, and steps scrubbed in preparation for the Season.

In fact, despite the chill, there was noise and bustle everywhere, from the blackbirds carolling on the rooftops to the hurrying servants in their new liveries in the streets below who were looking forward to the Season with all its promise of abundant food and extra money.

Everywhere, that is, except Number 67 Clarges Street.

The house at Number 67 seemed at first glance to be in mourning. The shutters were closed and its black, thin frontage stared down on the fashionable street like a gloomy undertaker. There were two iron hounds chained on the wide doorstep, gazing down at their paws as if they had long ago given up any hope of freedom. Although it was the fashion during each London Season to hire a house in Mayfair at a disproportionally high rent for sometimes very inferior accommodation, Number 67 stood empty and appeared likely to remain so, despite the fact that the rent was reasonable and the building in good repair.

The sad fact was that in an age when gambling fever ran high and everyone from a lord to a scullery maid was superstitious, Number 67 had been damned as 'unlucky'. And no mama hopeful of finding a good marriage for her daughter was going to risk incurring the wrath of those pagan gods who look down on the exclusive world of the top ten thousand.

The house was owned by the tenth Duke of Pelham, a young man, the ninth duke having hanged himself in the house in Clarges Street. The suicide of the ninth duke was not the only reason why the house had remained vacant for two Seasons and seemed likely to remain so for a third. One family, who had taken the house the Season after the duke's death, had lost all their money through their son's gambling. The family following that had suffered a worse fate. Their young and beautiful daughter, Clara, had been found dead in the middle of Green Park without a mark on her or anything to explain the cause of her death.

Although the present duke's agent advertised the town house at an increasingly modest rent, it stayed empty. The young duke was at Oxford University and did not appear over-concerned about the house, since it was only one of his many properties and he had a mansion of his own in Grosvenor Square.

The staff had been hired at very low wages during the old duke's time, and nothing had been done to alter this state of affairs as the young duke, who left the handling of everything to his agent, was not even aware that Number 67 had a permanent staff. Although the servants could barely eat on their wages, they had, when the house was first let, been able to supplement their diet and income by the many parties held there. The servants' table had groaned with leftover food, and livery and apron pockets had jingled with tips from the rich dinner guests. But without a tenant, their could be no alleviation of their sad state. So the servants of Number 67 gloomily looked on as their more fortunate rivals in the

3

neighbouring houses prepared for yet another lucrative few months.

The agent responsible for the hiring of the staff was a brute of a man called Mr Jonas Palmer. Palmer entered the servants' wages in his master's books at a high rate while paying them next to nothing. So far, the young duke had not asked to see the books, but Palmer knew that day would soon come and was prepared for it.

And not one of the servants could leave and find another position. For Palmer had a hold over all of them and wanted to keep them all exactly as they were, so that he could continue to cheat his master. In his many sets of books, locked carefully away where his young master would never find them, he had neatly recorded the actual wages he paid the staff and the details of their backgrounds, which he had carefully collected before hiring each one.

Mr John Rainbird, the butler, had been first footman in Lord Trumpington's household. He had been found in Lady Trumpington's bed and dismissed. Despite the fact that her ladyship seemed to be enjoying herself immensely when she was discovered, Rainbird had been discharged and sent out into the world with a bad reference. When Palmer had offered him the job of butler it had seemed too good to be true. The wages were very low and the old duke was a skinflint, but there were good pickings to be made during the Season and the Little Season, the old duke staying at Grosvenor Square but using the house in Clarges Street to

4

entertain. Because he had a morbid feeling that all his guests were thieves, he preferred to invite them to a house where the furniture and objets d'art were not very valuable. After the duke's death, Rainbird had found his wages cut to the bone. He had gone to Palmer to announce the termination of his employ. Palmer had said that if he did leave, then he, Palmer, would put a notice in the newspapers, warning all future employers of Rainbird's womanizing character. So Rainbird stayed. He was a slim, well-built man of forty with a clever comedian's face, sallow and mobile, a long chin, and a pair of sparkling grey eyes.

The cook, Angus MacGregor, who had been a sous chef in a noble milord's house in Paris just as the French Revolution broke out, had fled to England after watching his master beheaded. When it came to cooking, he was a genius, but his hot-headed Celtic temper had lost him one post after the other. He knew he would never get another post, much as he longed to take a cleaver to Palmer's fat neck. In his last job, he had thrown a leg of mutton at Lady Blessop after she had sent word down to the kitchens that the leg was badly cooked and that the chef was cheating her.

Housekeeper, Mrs Middleton – the 'Mrs' being a courtesy title – was a curate's daughter, genteel, educated, and fallen on hard times. Forced out into the world upon the death of her father, she had despaired of finding a ladylike post and thought the job as housekeeper at Number 67 had been heaven-sent.

Now, much as she wanted to leave, she knew that no one would employ her without a reference.

Footman, Joseph, tall and good-looking, had been dismissed from the Bishop of Burnham's palace for stealing, and although everyone knew privately the stealing was the result of the bishop's wife's penchant for lifting anything that took her fancy from the palace guests, her reputation had to be protected and so Joseph was told by the bishop that he might consider himself very lucky that he had not been sent to prison. Joseph was effeminate and adored the livery that first came with the job in Clarges Street. He could have left and taken a labouring job, but he was inordinately proud of his white hands and declared he would 'rather starve', which was what he was now almost doing.

Jenny, the chambermaid, small, quick, and dark, had found her first job at the tall house and could not possibly find another without a good reference. The same went for Alice, the tall, Junoesque housemaid, and the little drab of a between-stairs-cum-scullery-maid, Lizzie.

The pot boy, Dave, was a recent addition. He had run away from his master, a chimney sweep. He received no wages at all because it was Rainbird who had taken pity on the shivering waif when he had found him begging; Palmer did not know of Dave's existence. The staff at Clarges Street had become Dave's substitute family, and he never dreamt of leaving them.

On a cold spring night, they were all sitting in the

servants' hall, eating a modest meal of thin soup and stale bread. In palmier days, Rainbird and Mrs Middleton would retire to the housekeeper's little parlour halfway up the back stairs to take wine. Now they ate what was available with the other servants. Above their heads, the house crouched silent and empty, the rooms full of shrouded furniture.

Usually the servants were a united group – united in their burning resentment against the agent, Palmer. But that evening, the trouble started when the footman, Joseph, minced in from the street and threw himself sulkily down at the table.

'A pox on these street Arabs,' he said, holding up one shapely leg in its white silk stocking with the black clock.

'What did they do?' asked the Highland cook, MacGregor, spooning watery soup into a bowl.

'They stuck a pin in meh *calves* to see if they was *real*.' It was the custom of many footmen to wear wooden calves if Nature had not endowed them with the proper muscular legs considered *de rigueur* in a footman.

'And are they? Real, I mean,' said the cook, thumping the bowl of soup in front of Joseph.

'Course they're real, you great hairy *thing*. It's as well *you* aren't a footman. You would hehv to wear whole oak trees to make up for those spindle shanks of yours,' tittered Joseph. He picked up his spoon. 'Faugh! Whatever is this muck?'

'Mr MacGregor found a cat in the area,' giggled Jenny, the chambermaid.

'I'm no' takin' any mair insults,' said the Scotch cook. He picked up a roasting spit and advanced on Joseph.

'That's enough,' said Rainbird sharply. 'Go and put your head under the pump, Angus. As for you, Joseph, any more of your spite and we'll put you in skirts.'

'Jessamy,' sneered MacGregor.

'Just because eh hehv a certain elegance, a certain je ne sais quoi, there is no need to mock me.' Joseph took out a bottle of musk and held it delicately under his nose.

Mrs Middleton seized it. It spilled on the table and the pungent smell of musk mixed with the strong smell of old mutton from the soup.

'Where did you get this?' demanded Mrs Middleton. 'We are supposed to share our pennies for *food.*'

Dave, the pot boy, put a grubby finger in the spilled pool of scent, dabbed it behind his ears, and began to mince up and down. 'Look at me,' he said, one little hand on his bony hip. 'I'm Harriette Wilson.' Harriette Wilson was London's leading courtesan, dubbed by one and all The Queen of Tarts.

'Sit down,' said Alice, with a toss of her head. 'I'll take the birch to you, Dave, see if I don't.'

'There's to be no spending money on anything but food,' said Rainbird sternly.

'I couldn't 'elp it,' wailed Joseph, a Cockney whine creeping into his voice. 'I 'ad to 'ave somethink to keep me spirits up. There's that footman, Luke, next door. They've got Lord and Lady Charteris coming and that means routs and parties an' lots o' vails. New livery 'e 'ad, too. Looks like a Bond Street Fribble, and so I told 'im. I *'ates* this. Dingy kitchen, dingy food, no fun. You don't *understand*.'

'You're always whining,' said MacGregor, who had still not forgiven the insult to his legs. 'Prettifying yourself is all *you* do while I go out and scrounge to try to find us something to eat. What of *my* art? I am the best chef in London and I cannae prove it. I hate all of ye . . .' He changed into Gaelic and, although no one else could understand what he was saying, it sounded even nastier than it might have in English.

Little Lizzie burst into tears and threw her apron over her head. Rainbird sighed. Lizzie was such a scrap of a thing. They all looked down on her, and yet they were fond of her in their different ways.

MacGregor stopped his cursing and removed his white linen skull cap, where he had hidden a piece of meat, and silently pushed it across the table to the sobbing Lizzie.

Joseph jammed the stopper back in the musk bottle. 'Have this, Liz,' he pleaded. 'Don't cry.'

'Stop that row,' said Rainbird sharply. 'We are all feeling out of sorts,' he said in a gentler tone of voice, as Lizzie hiccuped dolefully and lowered her apron.

'We never said things like that to each other before,' sobbed Lizzie. 'Will our luck *never* change?'

'Not likely to,' said Jenny, the chambermaid.

'We could pray,' said Lizzie.

'Silly child,' sighed Rainbird. 'I'm sure we've all prayed.'

'But proper-like,' said Lizzie, drying her eyes with her apron. 'I mean, in a real church.'

'If you mean the Roman Catholic church,' said Joseph stiffly, 'you are the only one of that faith here. The rest of us is too genteel.'

But Lizzie had got hold of the idea of prayer in church and somehow it seemed to cheer her. She clasped her hands together. 'Oh, Mr Rainbird, could I go to church this evening?'

'What! And leave me with the dishes?' demanded MacGregor.

'*Please*, Mr Rainbird.'

'There are only a few bowls to wash, Angus,' said Rainbird. 'You'd best take Joseph with you, Lizzie. It doesn't do for a female to be out in the streets alone.'

'Not me,' said Joseph hurriedly. 'I ain't a papist. What if some of the other footmen should see me going in?'

'I'll go myself,' said Lizzie. 'I'll pray proper. Our luck will change. You'll see.' She scampered out of the servants' hall, her wooden clogs making a tremendous racket.

Mrs Middleton shook her head. 'Poor deluded child,' she said. 'My dear father, God rest his soul, always told me we must accept what God sends us.'

'Well, it's a pity He sent us Palmer,' snapped Rainbird.

With her shawl thrown over her head, Lizzie hurried through the dark streets, her flying shadow dancing first before her and then behind in the feeble light of the parish lamps. Soon fashionable London was left behind and the streets became meaner and darker. Pausing only to crouch in the shadow of a doorway when she heard any drunken bloods approaching, Lizzie flew along, her clogs clattering on the pavement. She turned into Soho Square, giving a little sigh of relief as she saw the welcoming bulk of St Patrick's Church. In her hand, she clutched one treasured penny, enough to buy a candle.

Although she longed with all her heart to pray to God that Joseph might notice her, Lizzie thought of all the servants in Clarges Street and decided she must pray for their future welfare without thinking of anything for herself.

The church was quiet, apart from a few French emigres. Walking slowly so that her clogs would not make too much of a noise, Lizzie paid a penny for a candle and then went to a statue of the Virgin Mary that was near the altar. Lighting the candle, she placed it before the Virgin, sank to her knees, and prayed with all her heart that the curse would be removed from Number 67 Clarges Street and that they would have a tenant for the Season. She prayed for an hour, steadfastly thrusting all thoughts of Joseph away as soon as the tall figure of the footman crept into her mind.

At last she arose, crossed herself, and made her way out into the cold, blustery wind whipping down the narrow streets. Far above the sooty chimneys one tiny little star pricked the sky. Lizzie felt suddenly happy. She knew it was an omen. God had heard her prayers. Now all she had to do was wait.

She walked straight back to Clarges Street, her head held high. No longer did she hide in doorways. Little Lizzie felt an exaltation she had never known before.

When she walked down the dark area steps to the basement, she thought for one heart-stopping moment that her prayers had been answered immediately. There were wild sounds of merriment coming from the servants' hall. She pushed open the door and went in.

The servants all had glasses of brandy in their hands. They were wildly applauding the cook, who had placed two crossed skewers on the table and, with his long apron hitched up, was performing some weird Highland dance, demonstrating how his buckled shoes never touched either skewer, no matter how much he leapt or pranced.

'Come in, girl,' called Rainbird. 'Angus here was searching in the back of the cellars and found loose bricks in the wall, and behind them he found two bottles of good French brandy. Take a glass and join us. Your prayers have been answered.'

'I wouldn't pray for anything like *brandy*,' said Lizzie, much shocked. 'But don't worry, Mr Rainbird. Me and God have taken care of everything.'

Rainbird winked at Mrs Middleton and touched his forehead. Mrs Middleton smiled and nodded, her great white cap bobbing back and forth. 'Poor child,' she whispered. 'She really believes it.'

'Let her believe it,' said Rainbird. 'One of us may as well nourish a little hope. But it's going to be another long, empty, dreary Season. Nothing will change.'

ONE

An unforgiving eye, and a damned disinheriting countenance.

SHERIDAN, *SCHOOL FOR SCANDAL*

Far away in another part of the British Isles, however, events were taking place that would change the fortunes of Number 67 Clarges Street.

It had all started at the end of February when Mr Roderick Sinclair, a retired Scottish lawyer, learned the glad tidings of the death of his brother, Jamie.

At first, Mr Sinclair could hardly believe his luck. He was a fat, jovial, slovenly man, a bachelor, who had retired five years before to enjoy the remainder of his days in drinking away his savings. Mr Sinclair fully expected to die before he reached the age of sixty. But his sixtieth birthday had come and gone, leaving him in a small apartment in the Royal Mile in Edinburgh with very little money left and the prospect of the workhouse before him. His brother,

Jamie, a wine merchant, had saved all his life, only grudgingly parting with any penny. In this way he had amassed a great fortune and was as rich as Roderick Sinclair was now poor. Jamie had been tottering on the brink of death for years. Mr Sinclair had waited so long for Jamie to cross over into the undiscover'd country from whose bourn no traveller returns that he had quite given up hope.

But that very day he was on his road to see Jamie's lawyer, nursing a pounding head – for he had celebrated his brother's death up and down every tavern in the Old Town the previous night – determined to celebrate further with a restorative 'meridian' – the traditional gill of ale that was drunk every morning in the taverns when the bells of St Giles played out the half-past eleven. In fact, most of the citizens of Edinburgh drank from the gill bell to the drum that was sounded by the town guard at ten in the evening to warn all citizens to clear the streets and taverns and go to bed. The very fact that Mr Sinclair still lived in the Royal Mile was a sign that he was slowly sinking towards the River Tick.

For the New Town, which had sprung up on the other side of the North Bridge, had gradually drawn all the gentry and aristocrats out of their crumbling, noisy tenements and set them up in stately mansions far from the bustle of the Mile or High Street, which ran from the medieval castle squatting on top of its fourteen-hundred-foot pile of rocks down to the Palace of Holyrood a mile away at the east end – hence the name, the Royal Mile. On either side of the Mile stood gloomy tenements, built as far back as the sixteenth century and compressing between them a dark maze of sloping alleys and courtyards as dreary as dungeons.

Mr Sinclair could remember the days when the Mile would be crowded at this early hour with noblemen lurching homewards after a night's drinking at one of the Old Town's many clubs. But now only a few die-hard aristocrats remained. Most had learned to despise the democratic ways of sharing the same building with tailors and washer-women, preferring to live on the other side of the green gulf that lay at the bottom of the castle rock where the New Town had sprung up.

How much had Jamie left? Mr Sinclair picked his way through the filth of the pavement muttering sums of thousands and thousands of guineas over and over.

It was as he was passing St Giles Church that his conscience smote him. His brother was dead, and he, Roderick Sinclair, had so far not shed one single tear. He tried to conjure up some fond thoughts of Jamie, and found he could not. Jamie, the elder, had always tormented him as a child. Jamie had married the only woman that Roderick Sinclair had ever loved by buying up the mortgage on her mother's house and threatening to evict her if she did not marry him. Her name had been Catherine Campbell, and Roderick knew to this day that Jamie had never loved her, but had wanted her only out of spite. Well, poor Catherine had died young and left Jamie childless. Bad cess to the man. He was better off dead.

Mr Sinclair felt a sinister itching in his big toe. Gout! Ah well, with Jamie's money he would be able to afford the best of wines. Gout was surely caused by twopenny ale.

The lawyer's office was situated at the bottom of the Mile. Only when he was turning into the dark close that led into the building did Mr Sinclair realize he should have changed his clothes. He had fallen asleep in a chair in the early hours of the morning, still wearing his old-fashioned chintz coat and knee breeches. A splash of ale marred his left stocking and his cravat was covered with snuff stains – somewhere during the merry roistering he had mistaken it for his handkerchief. He could only hope the lawyer would consider his dress a sign of extreme grief.

Patting his wig and settling his bicorne more firmly on his head, he climbed the noisome stairs, stepping over two peacefully snoring drunks.

The lawyer's name was Mr Kneebone. Mr Sinclair thought it a prodigious funny sort of name and considered cracking a joke until he saw the lawyer's ancient, funereal face.

'Come in, Mr Sinclair,' said Mr Kneebone in sepulchral tones. 'Aye, it's a sad day. Mr Jamie was a kenspeckle figure in this town.'

'To be sure, to be sure,' said Mr Sinclair, rubbing his hands and looking hopefully at the pile of parchment on the lawyer's desk. 'You won't be wanting to prolong my grief, Mr Kneebone, so I humbly suggest you begin reading the will right away.'

Mr Kneebone looked disapprovingly at Mr Sinclair over the tops of his spectacles, gave a dry cough, and walked with maddening, creaking slowness round the other side of the desk and sat down.

Mr Sinclair settled himself in a battered armchair by the fireplace and waited to hear the good news.

At first, he could not really take in what the lawyer was saying. It appeared Jamie had left such and such a sum to one obscure charity, and such and such a sum to another. Mr Sinclair shook his heavy head like a bull plagued by flies as the reading of the will went on and on listing sums left to charities and no sound of his own name.

The sudden shadow of the workhouse seemed to loom over him. He interrupted the lawyer. 'Ahem, Mr Kneebone, does Jamie say naethin' about me?'

'Do you wish me to read only the bit that pertains to you?'

'Yes.'

'Very well, although I thought that all of your brother's charitable bequests would interest you. A very charitable man. Let me see . . .' He rattled the parchment while Mr Sinclair waited in an agony of apprehension. 'Ah, here I have it! "To my profligate brother, Roderick . . ."'

Mr Sinclair flushed. 'Aye was fond of a joke was Jamie,' he mumbled.

'"To my profligate brother, Roderick Sinclair,"' went on Mr Kneebone severely, '"I leave my ward, Miss Fiona Sinclair."'

'Who? What!'

'Miss Fiona Sinclair.'

'Who the deil's she?'

'If you had been in touch with your brother during the last years of his life, you would know that he took a young lady under his protection–'

'The dirty auld–'

'Mr Sinclair! Mr Jamie's motives were of the purest. The girl came from an orphanage of which he was one of the trustees.'

'Well, let's hope he left me some money to look after her with.'

'Not a penny.'

Mr Sinclair moaned and clutched his heart.

'I am afraid so. It was Mr Jamie's opinion that you would drink yourself to death were you left any money. This Fiona has been taught God-fearing ways, and he considered her sobering company to assist you in your declining years.'

'Brandy,' whispered Mr Sinclair.

'I do not touch or keep spirits. I can make you some tea.'

'Tea!' screamed Mr Sinclair, leaping to his feet. '*Tea!* I will tell you what you can do with your tea, sirrah! You can take your tea and . . .'

Children crowded round the open doorway, laughing at the sight of the fat old man telling Mr Kneebone to put his tea in a place where it would

19

cause him great discomfort. Mr Sinclair charged through them when he had finished abusing the lawyer and hurtled down the stairs, tears running down his fat cheeks.

All that long day, he cried and cried. By the time he had ended up in 'the coffin', that long, narrow room in John Dowie's tavern, he felt he could cry no more. His mind was made up. He would have one more drink and then take himself home, sling his belt over the ham hook on the rafters, and hang himself by the neck. Having come to that decision, he sadly ordered a bottle of the best claret and proceeded to demolish it.

There were two advocates at the other end of the long table. They had a copy of the English newspaper, *The Morning Post*, and were discussing the social column. 'We should hae been born women, Erchie,' said one of them. 'You only need to have a pretty face at the London Season and you can marry as much money as you want.' They went on to discuss other items.

Mr Sinclair finished his claret and lurched to his feet. His legs seemed like jelly, particularly the left one, which gave him a dipping sort of walk, but by feeling his way along the sides of the buildings with both hands above his head, rather in the manner of a mountaineer feeling his way along a high, narrow ledge in the Alps, he regained his own stair.

Hanging himself proved to be no easy matter. He was very drunk, although his brain seemed crystal clear. But he had double vision. And try as he might to sling his belt over the ham hook, he could not seem to pick the real hook out from the ghostly one, although he tried them both. He wondered vaguely if he might not have treble vision and if the real hook were hanging somewhere else.

He climbed down from the chair on which he had been standing to ponder the matter when there came a rattling at the tirling pin on the outside door. The idea of committing suicide without letting any of his drinking cronies know what he was planning to do suddenly seemed a weak sort of way to shuffle off this mortal coil, and so he tacked to the door.

He picked up a candle in its holder, vaguely noticing with some pride that his hand was rock steady, and swung open the door.

A vision of loveliness looked back at him. It curtsied low. It said in a sweet, lilting voice, 'An it please you, sir, I am Fiona Sinclair.'

TWO

Its very speed was a dangerous and heady novelty for the old-fashioned, and it was with some daring that people entered the vehicle which would take them swaying through the night at a speed of as much as fifteen miles an hour.

F. GEORGE KAY, *ROYAL MAIL*

Mr Sinclair struggled awake next morning. He knew that something really awful had befallen him the day before, and for a while he was content to lie in his bed and stare at the ceiling and keep memory at bay. His mouth felt like a gorilla's armpit, and his forehead, like a furnace.

But at last the full enormity of Jamie's will crashed down on his tortured head. That Jamie, who had successfully kept up the *appearance* of being charitable all his life, getting himself elected to this and that board of orphanage or poor house without parting with so much as a farthing, should actually, finally, give it all away to charity out of sheer malicious spite was too much. Mr Sinclair closed his eyes and groaned aloud.

And then a gentle hand bathed his fevered temples with cologne, and a quiet voice said, 'Lie still, sir. I have made you a dish of tea.'

Mr Sinclair knocked away the hand and struggled up against the pillows. He could not remember getting to bed. He remembered opening the door to the prettiest female he had ever seen, and after that everything was blank. Now the lovely vision was sitting beside his bed. Roderick Sinclair blinked and looked again. It was hard to believe she was real.

Fiona Sinclair was a dazzling Highland beauty with a creamy skin and thick black hair that shone with blue lights. Her large eyes with their heavy fringe of lashes were grey, clear, silvery grey. She was wearing an old-fashioned gown with the waist where a woman's waist should be instead of the current fashion, which put it up under the armpits. Her waist was tiny, her bosom perfect.

'How did I get to bed?' asked Mr Sinclair, saying the first thing that came into his head.

'You fell on the floor,' said Fiona calmly. 'I put you to bed.'

Mr Sinclair felt down his large body and found it clothed only in his dirty nightshirt. He blushed for the first time in years. 'You've got a good back on ye if you could lift the likes of me,' he said, trying to sound as hearty and avuncular as possible.

Fiona sat quietly, her hands in her lap. Her hands were long fingered and very white.

How beautiful she is, thought Mr Sinclair. How

utterly useless! He could practically see the work-house walls closing in on him. A thought struck him. 'I'm surprised a lassie like you could make her way here without all the lads in Edinburgh sniffing at her heels.'

'I covered my head and the most of my face with the hood of my cloak,' said Fiona. 'Mr Jamie told me I was so ugly that people stared at me, and I do not like to be stared at.'

'You're the most beautiful creature I've ever seen,' said Mr Sinclair bluntly. 'Jamie must have wanted you for hisself.'

A tiny frown marred the perfection of Fiona's brow.

'Never mind,' went on Mr Sinclair. 'I have something to do that's private. Why don't you go back to my brother's?'

'I cannot,' said Fiona. 'The house was left to an orphanage, and so I was turned out.'

'That's not possible,' said Mr Sinclair hotly. 'The funeral's only tomorrow.'

'Mr Jamie told the orphanage that they might take over the minute he died. He told them I had been provided for.'

'Oh, he did, did he?' snarled Mr Sinclair. 'What exactly was your relationship with Jamie?'

'I beg your pardon, sir?'

'To put it bluntly, were you substitute daughter or mistress?'

'Oh, no, I am too ugly to have deserved either position. Mr Jamie told me so. He was rescuing me from myself. He said he saw harlotry in my eyes.'

'He was looking in his ain mirror, the dirty auld miser.'

'I beg your pardon?'

'God grant me patience. Look, I have very little money. I cannot keep you.'

'Very well,' said Fiona equably.

'So you will need to find work.'

'Yes,' said Fiona. She gave him a sudden, dazzling smile. Mr Sinclair blinked.

The gill bell sounded. He had a longing to escape this problem, to go back to the tavern for one last meridian. Then he would need to send her away somewhere so that he could hang himself. He would scrawl a will on a bit of paper leaving her the apartment and its contents.

'Leave me,' he said curtly. 'Take away the tea. I am going to get dressed.'

She rose, curtsied, and glided from the room. Mr Sinclair wondered what she was thinking, and finally came to the conclusion that she thought about very little.

His clothes felt different. He realized his coat had been sponged and pressed and his shirt and cravat were white and crisp. How she had managed to achieve all these miracles during the night, he could not fathom. But his morale was rising with the unaccustomed feel of fresh linen next to his skin.

When he emerged from his bedroom, it was to find his small parlour shining like a new pin. The brass fender in front of the blazing fire shone like gold. The room smelled clean and fresh. In a sudden burst of gratitude Mr Sinclair said, 'Hey, lassie, put on your cloak and I'll take ye for a dram.'

She obediently put on her cloak and then dragged the hood over her head so that it concealed most of her features.

'There's no need for that,' said Mr Sinclair. 'Put your hood back. You are fair to look on.'

'But Mr Jamie said–'

'Tish! Cunning Jamie knew you were a diamond of the first water, but he didn't want you to know it.'

Again, that puzzled little frown. But she obediently put back her hood. The cloak was an old, blue woollen one, but her dazzling looks seemed to turn the cloth to velvet. Mr Sinclair felt his heartbeats quicken. It was decades since he had had a pretty woman on his arm.

Their progress down the Royal Mile caused a sensation. Men stood dead in their tracks and stared open-mouthed. Carriages jammed the narrow street. Drivers stood up on the boxes of their coaches and craned their necks for a last glimpse of Fiona Sinclair as she tripped along daintily by Mr Sinclair's side.

The day was windy, but there was a faint, warm promise of spring in the air. Bursting with pride, Mr Sinclair ushered Fiona into John Dowie's tavern.

Now, although quite respectable ladies had frequented the taverns in his youth, a new wave of gentility had put paid to such free and easy democracy, and there were only men in the narrow room when Mr Sinclair entered with Fiona on his arm – men who rose to their feet.

'Sit down!' bawled Mr Sinclair, embarrassed. 'Have ye no' seen a lassie afore?'

The gentlemen slowly sank back down into their seats and went on staring. Mr Sinclair ordered a bottle of claret. There was no use in saving money now that he meant to end it all. But, somehow, yesterday's despair seemed to have fled. Fiona delicately sipped her claret.

'How did you come to live with Jamie?' asked Mr Sinclair, forgetting all the staring eyes in the pleasure of his first sip of wine.

'I was at the orphanage, and Mr Jamie was one of the trustees. The governor of the orphanage informed me one day that Mr Jamie had adopted me as his ward and I was to go with him and be a good girl and learn my scriptures.'

'And was he kind to you?'

'Oh, yes, very kind. He would read me the scriptures and make me pray to God to bear the burden of my ugliness.'

'My dear girl, you're beautiful.'

'You are the only person who thinks so, and it is very kind of you to lie.'

'I'm not lying,' howled Mr Sinclair. He lowered his voice. 'Jamie didn't . . . well . . . touch you in any way?'

'Yes.'

'Michty me! Worse than I thought.'

'He would sometimes stroke my hair and call me his poor child.'

'And that's all?'

'Of course. Did you mean anything else?'

Mr Sinclair pulled his handkerchief out of his pocket, noticed with vague surprise that it was clean, and mopped his forehead. 'No, no,' he said.

His eye fell on the copy of *The Morning Post* that had been left on the tavern table by the two advocates. He idly turned the pages, remembering vaguely what they had said about the London Season.

His mouth fell open as an idea hit him. He looked at Fiona and back at the paper, and then back at Fiona again. How wonderful it would be if Jamie, looking down from heaven, or more probably up from hell, could see that his bequest had turned into a fortune after all!

There was no doubt that a girl of such exquisite beauty as Fiona could take London by storm. Mr Sinclair began to perspire, and thoughts, hopes, and ambitions crowded into his head.

But no one on earth, that is, no one worth knowing, would call on a girl who lived in some cheap part of town. He turned the paper over and over, abstractedly reading the advertisements, only half taking in what he read. And then, all at once, one advertisement seemed to leap up out of the page.

A House for The Season
Gentleman's residence, 67,
Clarges Street, Mayfair.
Furnished town house. Trained
servants. Rent: £80 sterling.
Apply, Mr Palmer, 25, Holborn.

Mr Sinclair had visited London several times when he was a young man. He knew Clarges Street and knew that the rent, although it might seem enormous to some, was in fact ridiculously cheap for a town house in Mayfair. If he sold his own apartment, say, and everything in it, he could raise just enough to take Fiona to London for a Season. *Then*, if nothing came of it, he would hang himself.

He looked at Fiona. She sat there, vague, calm, and extraordinarily beautiful. He realized with alarm that this treasure was being exposed to the vulgar gaze of what seemed like the half of Edinburgh, since more and more men had crowded into the tavern to stare at Fiona.

'Come along,' he said, leaving a bottle of wine unfinished for the first time in his life.

The gentlemen of the tavern fell back as if before royalty as he led Fiona out. He could feel notes being thrust into his pockets, and knew they would all be from men begging permission to call on him. But *his* Fiona should go to the highest bidder. Why waste such sweetness on some mere shopkeeper or advocate? Any Scotchman with *real* money went to London for the Season.

Followed by an admiring throng, Mr Sinclair led Fiona back home, doing mathematical sums in his head. Then he became aware that several of the gentlemen had broken out of their stupefied trance and were pressing forward, thrusting flowers and notes on Fiona. Mr Sinclair scowled horribly. He was desperate now to send an express letter to this man Palmer. The coach only took forty-five and a half hours to reach London, the Royal Mails being so fast some people would not journey on them for fear of a seizure caused by travelling at fifteen miles per hour.

'Put your hood up,' he ordered sharply, as more admirers pressed around.

Fiona obeyed. 'I told you I was ugly,' she said.

A blackbird flew down the chimney of Number 67 Clarges Street and batted the walls with its sooty wings, looking for a way out. Before MacGregor could slaughter the bird, Lizzie seized it up, ran to the kitchen door, and let it out. It flew straight up to the roof of the house opposite, and, after a few moments, shook out its sooty wings and began to sing.

Lizzie stood with her hands clasped until Mac-Gregor told her sharply to scrub down the walls as a punishment for her folly. Lizzie turned a radiant face up to the cook. 'It's an omen,' she breathed. 'This house has been let. I *feel* it.'

'Havers,' said the cook sourly. But some old superstitious fear stirred in his Highland blood, and he kept clear of little Lizzie for the rest of the day.

Hectic weeks followed for Mr Sinclair. Some drunken Highland laird with more money than sense paid him handsomely for his apartment in which said Highland laird meant to house his new mistress.

Mr Sinclair had not attended his brother's funeral. The fact was noted in a report in an Edinburgh newspaper. It seemed appalling that such a great philanthropist as Mr Jamie Sinclair should go to his grave unmourned by his only brother.

During all the bustle of preparation, Mr Sinclair had not really time to find out what went on behind Fiona's placid brow. She had accepted the decision to move to London with the same tranquillity as she accepted everything. Mr Sinclair, when he thought of her at all, decided she was somewhat touched in her upperworks, but none the worse for that, since it was well known that the aristocracy did not favour clever women.

By the time he had paid for two inside seats on the Mail and had sent a deposit of £25 to Mr Palmer – dispatching the latter without even waiting for Mr Palmer's letter of acceptance – Mr Sinclair calculated that he had £800 left. Gamblers in London, he knew, could lose as much as £800 or more on the throw of a die. It would not go very far. He would need to rack his brains for a plan to launch Fiona without actually putting his hand in his pocket. He had the right address. All he needed was a scheme.

Beautiful as Fiona was, without stability, riches, or family in her background, she might either be offered the post of someone's mistress or have to marry the first man who asked her. Mr Sinclair felt he owed her more than that. She would have to marry to justify the expense, but he wanted the girl to have a choice.

He had never had much luck with the cards, but, in the hope that he might improve his performance, he practised nightly with Fiona, teaching her how to play piquet, silver loo, whist, hazard dice, and faro. But he came to the conclusion that the idea of gambling was hopeless because Fiona – who, anyone could see, had little brain – managed to beat him every time. He decided to shelve the problem until they were on the road. He had found in the past that the swaying motion of the coach activated his mind wonderfully.

'Who has called?' asked Lizzie, opening the kitchen window to let in the first breath of spring air.

'It's Mr Palmer, and get on with your work,' said the housekeeper, Mrs Middleton.

'God rot his black heart,' muttered MacGregor.

'Mr Rainbird is with him upstairs,' said Mrs Middleton fussily. 'Alice, take that tray up to the drawing room. Have we no cakes or biscuits?'

'No,' growled the cook, 'and if we had, I wouldnae be wastin' them on Palmer.'

Alice straightened the cap on her blond hair and went out carrying the tray with maddening slowness. Everything the stately Alice did was slow and studied. When she came back, Mrs Middleton looked at her anxiously. 'How are things?'

Alice shrugged, a long, slow sort of shrug that seemed to go on forever. 'Mr Palmer is reminding Mr Rainbird that he is tied to this house forever,' she said.

'Oh, dear, *poor* Mr Rainbird,' said Mrs Middleton. 'Now he'll be in *such* a temper. Has Jenny done the bedrooms?'

'What is there to be done?' asked Alice. 'It's hard cleaning and dusting when there ain't nobody to clean and dust for.'

'Isn't anybody,' corrected Mrs Middleton primly.

Alice gave her a slow look of surprise. 'Now didn't I just say that?'

Mrs Middleton went to take down the canister of Bohea; the little Hysop tea there was being saved for high days and holidays. She felt sure Mr Rainbird would be in the need of something sustaining. Mr Palmer had no doubt called only to enjoy the exercising of his power.

Half an hour passed before they heard Rainbird's step on the stairs. He burst into the kitchen, his eyes sparkling. 'The house is let,' he cried. He seized Mrs Middleton and began to dance about the kitchen with her.

'Let!' gasped Mrs Middleton, clutching her cap.

MacGregor dropped a pot.

'What's to do?' demanded Joseph languidly, appearing at the kitchen door.

'The house has been let, let, *let!*' sang Rainbird.

Jenny burst into the kitchen, the streamers of her cap flying. 'Did you say *let?*'

Rainbird nodded. The staff fell on each other, hugging and kissing. Lizzie tried to hug Joseph, but he pushed her away.

'Who to?' they all demanded.

'A Scotchman and his ward,' said Rainbird. 'A Mr Sinclair. Oh, the parties and routs, the food, the guineas. Mayhap we'll all get new clothes should he prove generous.'

'I knew my prayers would be answered,' said Lizzie.

'Yes,' said Rainbird slowly. 'Yes ... that's right, Lizzie.'

A silence fell on the group while they looked at Lizzie with something approaching awe.

Mr Sinclair was glad to note there were no susceptible young men in the mail coach. The other two inside occupants were a thin spinster lady and a tired-looking middle-aged lawyer's clerk. The passengers on the roof were sedate and middle-aged.

The coachman cracked his whip, and the black and maroon Royal Mail coach moved off. Mr Sinclair had never travelled by the mail coach before, and he was awed and exhilarated by the speed.

So elated was Mr Sinclair, in fact, that he found it hard to think. The gentle rocking of the slow regular coach he had taken in the past had made thought easy. But it was hard to worry about anything as they dashed through the countryside and one triumphant blast of the horn sent a cheeky goodbye flying back to the looming black tenements of Edinburgh.

After several hours and several changes of horses, he became accustomed to the speed, but instead of thinking, he fell fast asleep. It was the slowing of the hectic pace that awoke him. He assumed they must be approaching another inn. But by the light of the carriage lamps, he could see they were now going through a white world.

'Snow,' he thought, cursing under his breath. If they had to spend the night at an inn, he did not feel like breaking into his precious hoard of money in order to pay for two bedchambers. He leaned sideways and whispered to Fiona. 'If we have to rack up for the night somewhere, would you mind sleeping on a chair?'

'No,' said Fiona placidly. 'I can sleep anywhere.'

Mr Sinclair experienced a sudden rush of affection for her. Through all the hurly-burly of the leaving arrangements, she had remained as calm and as beautiful as ever. She was travelling in the same clothes she had worn when she had first arrived on his doorstep. He had been appalled to learn that she had very little else, her sole wardrobe being made up of two wool gowns and two cotton gowns, all made sometime in the last century, along with carefully darned shifts and stockings and one pair of shoes. Jamie had obviously found her clothes among the donations to some of his charities. But Mr Sinclair had told her she must make do with what she had until they reached London, as the latest thing the Edinburgh shops had to offer might prove to be sadly provincial.

The coach fumbled its way on through the blizzard. 'I am paying good money to get to London,' said the sharp-faced spinster. 'I was told the Royal Mail could travel in any weather.'

'We are still travelling, madam,' said the lawyer's clerk wearily. 'Those poor people on the roof must be frozen.'

'This is a weird spring.' Mr Sinclair shivered.

The coach creaked to a halt and then dipped and swayed as the coachman climbed down from the box. He wrenched open the door, and the spinster let out a shriek of protest when a small snowstorm whirled into the interior of the carriage.

'Can't go any further,' said the coachman. 'There's gates up ahead. Gentleman's residence, most like. See if they'll take us in. It's fifteen mile to the nearest inn, and we'll never make it in this.'

'Where are we?' asked Mr Sinclair.

'Liddle bit north of the border, I reckon.' The coachman slammed the door just as the spinster was about to protest.

'Well, *reelly!*' she bridled. 'I shall put in a strong complaint.'

Fiona rubbed the misted glass with her sleeve and looked out at the swirling whiteness in delighted wonder. Mr Sinclair realized again that he knew very little about her and had not even bothered to ask. Did she know her parents? She had been given the name Sinclair by Jamie. What had been her family name?

The coach swayed and dipped and lurched as it swung off the road. 'I hope this will work,' said Mr Sinclair. 'If it's a grand mansion, we might be sent to the right-about.'

'*I* am a lady,' said the spinster, flashing a malicious look at Fiona, 'although others may not be.'

'That is quite enough of that,' said the lawyer's clerk in the quavering voice of a timid man determined to assert himself.

The spinster sniffed, but relapsed into silence.

The coach finally stopped in front of a large mansion. A lamp was hanging over the entrance portico. The coachman climbed down and rang the bell.

A powdered, liveried footman came out on the step. He retreated and was replaced by an imposing-looking butler. The butler shook his head. The coachman waved his arms. Inside the coach, they could not hear what was being said, but no one wanted to open the window and risk losing the little warmth they had.

The butler retired and then reappeared with a tall gentleman beside him. The gentleman had a weak, dissipated face that was rouged and painted. He was exquisitely dressed, and his fair hair was teased into a miraculous array of tangled and artistically disarrayed curls. He listened with a listless, bored air to the coachman's tale and then said something to the butler.

The coachman came back towards the carriage, rubbing his hands. He pulled open the door and said cheerfully, 'We can spend the night in the kitchens, so we'll have food and warmth.'

'Whose place is it?' asked Mr Sinclair.

'Gentleman by the name of Pardon.'

Pardon. Mr Sinclair frowned. There was something about that name, something unsavoury connected with it. He looked uneasily at Fiona's innocent face and felt inadequate for the first time. He felt he should never have brought such a ewe lamb out into the cold world.

Huddled together, the inside and outside passengers trooped into the entrance hall, clutching their belongings. The hall was wood-panelled and hung with portraits. A fire burned in a marble fireplace, and the air was scented with rose water.

'This way,' said the butler, leading the way to the back of the hall so that he could conduct these plebeian guests down to the kitchens.

Mr Pardon stood in front of the fireplace, warming his bottom, the tails of his evening coat hitched up. 'Serve dinner, Johnson,' he called to his butler. 'My guests are sharp set.'

'Very good, sir,' said the butler. 'I will usher these persons belowstairs first.'

The passengers shuffled through the hall, gazing

about them in awe, all except Fiona, who seemed unaware of her surroundings. She drew back the hood of her cloak and shook out her hair.

'By George,' muttered Mr Pardon. Something made Mr Sinclair take Fiona's arm and draw it protectively through his own.

His languid pose completely gone, Mr Pardon glided forward and intercepted Mr Sinclair and Fiona. 'My apologies,' he said smoothly. 'I was not aware a *gentleman* was of the party. Allow me to introduce myself. My name is Pardon, Percival Pardon.'

'Roderick Sinclair,' said Mr Sinclair, executing a clumsy bow.

'And this . . . ?' asked Mr Pardon, smiling at Fiona. Before Mr Sinclair could speak, Fiona said, 'I am Fiona Sinclair, Mr Sinclair's daughter.'

THREE

... his legs were so beautiful ... his skin so clear and transparent ... Really all these things, and thirty thousand a year besides, were enough to melt a heart of stone.

HARRIETTE WILSON'S MEMOIRS

Mr Sinclair blinked, wondering why she had not said she was his ward, but quickly decided Fiona was being simple-minded as usual.

'Charming,' said Mr Pardon. His pale eyes studied Fiona's face and figure in a way that Mr Sinclair did not like. 'Of course you must join me for dinner.' Mr Pardon snapped his fingers. 'James,' he said to a tall footman, 'tell Mrs Anderson to have ... let me see ... the Yellow Room and the Blue Room made ready for Mr and Miss Sinclair and set dinner back by half an hour.'

'We are honoured, sir,' said Mr Sinclair, still holding tightly on to Fiona. 'But I fear we are putting you to too much trouble.'

'Nonsense, my dear Sinclair. You will not be my only unexpected guests. The Earl of Harrington has also thrown himself on my . . . er . . . mercy, having been travelling south when the storm struck.'

Mr Sinclair had a longing to say he would be quite happy in the kitchens with the other passengers, but the housekeeper had appeared and was obviously waiting to conduct them upstairs. All he could do was to bow and thank Mr Pardon, resolve to caution Fiona, and hope she might grasp at least a tenth of what he was saying.

The house was richly carpeted. Ornaments and statues gleamed in the soft light of oil lamps. Fiona was given the Yellow Room. The Blue Room was next door. A footman put their scanty luggage on the floor and said he would send a maid to see to their unpacking.

'No need,' said Mr Sinclair hastily. He turned to the housekeeper. 'If you will excuse us, mistress, I wish to have a word with my wa– daughter.'

The housekeeper and footman left.

'Sit down, Fiona,' said Mr Sinclair. 'It's time we had a talk.'

Fiona took off her cloak and sat down by the fire. The room was very warm. It was dominated by a large modern bed that had the bedposts left bare and supporting an elaborately domed top. Thick yellow silk curtains hung at the window. The mantelpiece was of marble and, to the right of the fire, a mahogany tallboy soared up to the shadows of the ceiling. There was a bowl of rose petals on a satinwood dropside table, sending their delicate summer scent into the quiet, still air of the room.

'Now,' said Mr Sinclair, 'why did you call yourself my daughter?'

'I thought it . . . more fitting,' said Fiona after a pause.

'Well, so it is, so it is. It had not crossed my mind that as my ward people would wonder why you were not chaperoned, and with a predator like Pardon around, it is as well to observe the conventions. Make sure he does not get you alone.'

Fiona nodded, her eyes very large and limpid.

'What is your real name, Fiona? I assume my brother gave you his name.'

'Yes. I do not know my real name. The orphanage called me Fiona Ross because it was a Mr Ross who found me.'

'Found you . . . where?'

'Outside St Giles Church.'

'Then you should have gone to the Foundling Hospital.'

'I did. I was kept there until I was seven and then sent to the orphanage so that I might be trained as a servant. The Foundling Hospital called me Fiona. The orphanage added the Ross.'

'And why weren't you sent out as a servant? It is unusual for the orphanage to keep you so long.'

'I was employed at the orphanage, cleaning and cooking. Mr Sinclair took me home with him when I was thirteen.'

'And how old are you now?'

'Eighteen . . . I think.'

'So Jamie had ye all that time and never a word to me!'

Fiona said nothing.

Mr Sinclair rose to his feet, went to the window, pulled back the curtain and peered out. 'Rain,' he said with satisfaction. 'The mail won't wait here longer than necessary. We'd best fix ourselves for dinner as best we may. Leave the talking to me. I'll apologize for our dress – say we've sent the bulk of our wardrobe on to London. Knock at my door in about ten minutes and I'll take you down.'

Fiona nodded again. When he left, she was still sitting by the fire, gazing dreamily into the flames.

As Mr Sinclair scrambled into a rusty black evening coat, which he had bought ten years before, and was now two sizes too small for him, he kept thinking of Fiona, sitting by the fire. The full enormity of what he was doing struck him like a hammer blow. How could he take such an innocent girl and put her up on the block of the marriage market like a cow at Smithfield?

He thought of the past few weeks, of how pleasant it had been to dress in clean linen and eat good food and sit in the evening in a shining apartment. Surely he could have managed somehow. He could have started up his law practise again, drunk less, worked hard. It was greedy folly to pin his hopes on one soft-headed girl.

He worried and worried, and the sight of Fiona when she knocked and entered his room jabbed his conscience afresh. She was wearing her other wool gown, which was of a dull crimson colour and old-fashioned cut. The sleeves were long and tight to the wrist, which at least made up for her lack of gloves.

To his surprise, she had piled the masses of her black hair up on top of her head, letting only a few stray curls dangle from the knot on top. She looked quite regal and Mr Sinclair began to hope that her outstanding beauty would stop the members of the dinner party from noticing the poverty of her dress. Good God! They might think him a miser!

'You look very beautiful, Fiona,' he said, patting her arm before drawing it through his own.

She smiled at him, but there was a flicker of something in her large grey eyes that looked almost like cynicism. It was so fleeting, darting as it did like a gleaming fish in the shallows, that Mr Sinclair thought he must have been mistaken.

A footman was waiting in the passage outside to escort them downstairs. The guests, he said, had already taken their places at table.

Pardon, thought Mr Sinclair again. There was something about him not so long ago . . . something involving a servant girl found dead in odd circumstances.

The footman held open a door, and the noise of voices gusted out into the rich quiet of the house. Mr Sinclair entered the dining room with Fiona on his arm. There was a sudden hush. He was aware of two rows of staring eyes, and his arm tightened on Fiona's.

'I told you so,' said Mr Pardon to the world at large. He walked forward. 'Mr Sinclair, you take the seat over there next to Mrs Hudson. Miss Sinclair, beside Lord Harrington if you please.'

Mr Sinclair groaned inwardly. He would have liked to have kept Fiona next to him.

He sat down next to a richly dressed buxom matron and prayed for a quick thaw so that the coach might be able to leave early in the morning.

There were twelve people including himself and Fiona. The men were beautifully tailored, and the women blazed with jewellery. Their eyes were hard and assessing. There was no way in which he was now going to find courage to apologize for his dress.

This, then, was the world into which he, Roderick Sinclair, planned to make his debut. He took only a small sip of excellent claret and left the rest in his glass. Had he drunk less, he might not be in this predicament. People such as these would never accept him, beautiful 'daughter' or no. Mrs Hudson had given him one cold, raking look and then had turned to the gentleman on her other side. The lady on his right had not even favoured him with so much as a glance.

He looked down the table to where Fiona sat next to the Earl of Harrington, and took small comfort from the fact that the earl in his way did not belong to this decadent company either.

He was a tall man in his thirties with a high-nosed handsome face. The exquisite line of his tailored coat and the snowy intricacy of his cravat made every other man look overdressed. He had a tanned face and hair as black as Fiona's, only his eyes were like those of a hawk, a peculiar yellowish topaz. He was talking politely to Fiona in a bored sort of way.

Mr Sinclair thanked God for small mercies. Lord Harrington was obviously the only man in the room who was completely unaffected by Fiona's beauty. The rest were frankly goggling, and the ladies were sulking and bridling as they failed to claim the attention of their dinner partners.

Mr Pardon's eyes, thought Mr Sinclair, were like two snails. It was as if they crawled all over Fiona's body, leaving a slimy trail. Pardon had a lady on either side of him, but he never once took his eyes from Fiona's face and figure. Mr Sinclair could only be glad she was at the far end of the table.

With Mr Rainbird leading the way, the small staff of 67 Clarges Street turned into Soho Square. Soon a small forest of candles was burning before the statue of the Virgin in St Patrick's Church.

'Hope this isn't a waste of money,' muttered Joseph as they all shuffled out again after having said their prayers.

'How can you say that, Mr Joseph?' cried Lizzie, much shocked. 'It was God who sent us the tenants. I prayed for them, too, for Mr Sinclair and his ward.'

'Why pray for *them*?' sniffed Joseph. 'It's us what needs the 'elp . . . help.'

'But I prayed for them to have a safe journey,' said Lizzie. ''Cos if anythink happens to them, happen *we* won't have a tenant after all.'

They all looked at Lizzie in surprise. 'Mayhap we'd better say a prayer for them, too,' said Rainbird.

Rather self-consciously, they all shuffled back into the church.

'What are you thinking about?' demanded the Earl of Harrington sharply. He was not used to dealing with any lady who seemed as utterly uninterested in him as this hen-witted provincial.

'I was admiring the sideboard,' said Fiona.

'I have never been cast in the shade by a sideboard before,' said the earl.

'Yes, it is certainly large enough.'

'Large enough for what?'

'To cast a shadow.'

'My dear Miss Sinclair, what I meant . . . never mind. What is so fascinating about that particular sideboard?'

'It is so efficient,' said Fiona dreamily. 'There is one urn for drinking water and one for washing water. There is a warming cupboard and a cellarette and drawers for knives and forks, and . . .' Her eyes fell on the rows of chamberpots underneath, placed there for the convenience of the gentlemen after dinner.

'You are easily entertained, Miss Sinclair.'

'Yes, I am,' said Fiona simply. 'But why are the knives and forks washed there, and not in the kitchen?'

'Because, no doubt, the kitchens are very far away.'

'Why?'

'Because one does not want the servants underfoot.'

'But the food gets cold if the kitchens are far away and the staff must work harder, so no one benefits.'

'In your own mansion,' said Lord Harrington tartly, 'no doubt you have the kitchen in your drawing room.'

It almost looked as if Miss Sinclair were trying to stifle a laugh.

'When your mind was wholly on the sideboard, Miss Sinclair,' pursued Lord Harrington, 'I asked you twice why you were travelling to London.'

'For the Season,' answered Fiona.

'Indeed!' His yellow gaze flicked down the table to where Mr Sinclair sat with the candlelight illuminating the shine on his old black coat and then returned to Fiona in her old wool gown. 'An expensive business, the Season,' he said meditatively.

'So I believe,' said Fiona. 'But I shall marry someone very rich, so it won't matter.'

'It is not so easy to marry someone rich unless you are rich yourself,' he said sharply. 'The aristocracy are famous for making profitable marriages.'

'What makes you think we are not rich?' asked Fiona in surprise.

'My dear young lady, you force me to be impolite. You are not dressed in a manner to suggest you have any money at all.'

'That is what I told Papa,' said Fiona, watching with interest as the dessert was borne to the table. It was a model of a snow-capped mountain with the small figure of a man on top made out of angelica and blancmange. Its slopes were lapped by a sea of milk punch. 'Papa says,' went on Fiona, 'that a somewhat dowdy appearance might repel fortune hunters. Papa is monstrous afraid of fortune hunters.'

At that moment, Mr Sinclair looked down the table, obviously wondering what his ward was talking about. Fiona threw him a dazzling smile.

'Of course,' went on Fiona blithely, 'Papa is a very great miser, and *I* think he merely says all that about fortune hunters to excuse his penny pinching.'

'You are very frank, Miss Sinclair.'

Fiona looked at him wide-eyed. 'Lord Harrington,' she said severely, 'you would not wish me to *lie.*'

'My wishes should not concern you. But I would advise you to be more discreet in your conversation when you reach London.'

'Why?'

'It might give the gentlemen a disgust of you.'

'Well, they will probably have that it any case. I am quite ugly, you know.'

'Nonsense. You are the most beautiful woman I ever beheld.'

'How kind of you to say so. But your air of barely suppressed boredom gives the lie to your compliment.'

'I do not lie, Miss Sinclair.'

'Then why is the truth unfashionable for me and fashionable for you?'

The answer to that one was, 'Because I am the Earl of Harrington and you are a Scottish nobody,' but Lord Harrington felt even the naive Miss Sinclair would consider him a complete coxcomb if he said it.

'I find it too difficult to explain at the moment. Tell me,' he said quickly, seeing another 'why' forming on Fiona's perfect mouth, 'do you read much?'

'Not of late. I like reading poetry.'

'Ah, the romantic poets, no doubt.'

'Yes, I like poetry,' said Fiona as if he had not spoken. 'Sometimes what I read seems very apt.' Her clear gaze flew to where Mr Pardon was sitting at the other end of the table and she said softly, 'This painted child of dirt that stinks and stings.'

'Surely you do not refer to our host?'

'I think Mr Pope was referring to Lord Hervey,' said Fiona seriously. 'I do not think Mr Pardon was alive at the time Mr Pope wrote that.'

'No,' he agreed, looking at her curiously. 'A fact, I am sure, of which you are well aware.'

'Of course,' laughed Fiona. 'Did I not just say so?'

But Lord Harrington had been sure, just for one split second, that Miss Sinclair had cast the quotation in the direction of Mr Pardon. He glanced down at her face. It was marred by a slightly stupid expression. Miss Sinclair was as hen-witted as she was beautiful. A pity. Yet she would not be short of admirers in London. He knew he was unusual in that he liked ladies, however young and pretty, to be intelligent.

She had attracted and held Lord Harrington's attention too long to please the other ladies present. Two of them, Mrs Hudson and a Lady Miles, were married. A third, Mrs Jemima Leech, a widow, was Mr Pardon's current mistress, as highly painted and cold-eyed as he was himself. But the two remaining ladies were a Miss Giles-Denton and a Miss Plumtree. Miss Harriet Giles-Denton was a soft blonde whose features seemed to have been made out of marshmallow. Miss Bessie Plumtree was a small, wiry brunette with angry pointed elbows and an air of perpetual outrage on her pointed, sallow face. Both had gone into raptures at the unexpected arrival of Lord Harrington. They lived locally and were being chaperoned on their visit by Mrs Hudson, who had assured their respective mamas that Mr Pardon was good *ton*, no matter what anyone might say, and his friendship would benefit both girls during their coming Season.

Both Harriet and Bessie now remembered how warmly Lord Harrington had smiled on them before dinner, reading passion into every cool civility and damning Miss Fiona Sinclair as a very common, bold type of hussy. That she should have attracted the attentions of Mr Pardon was not surprising. For Mrs Hudson had warned them that Mr Pardon was *very* wicked, but had added that unfortunately in society one must cultivate the wicked along with the good in order to ensure a firm foothold on the social ladder. It was *surmised* that Mrs Leech was Mr Pardon's mistress, but Mrs Hudson had told them that because he was a bachelor and because Mrs Leech was not exactly living with him, there was nothing about that liaison to bring a blush to the most modest cheek.

Until the arrival of Lord Harrington, the house party had seemed prodigiously dull to the two young hopeful debutantes, the only other marriageable man besides their host being an inarticulate army captain with large feet.

Both resolved to put Miss Sinclair well and truly in her place just as soon as they retired to the drawing room. Mr Sinclair, morose over his untouched wine, read that resolve in their faces, saw the way they looked daggers at Fiona, and was determined to save his ward from embarrassment.

Lord Harrington had turned to talk to Lady Miles, feeling he had been paying Miss Sinclair more attention than was good for her. He sensed, rather than saw, that Fiona was happily engaged in entertaining the stammering captain. After some time, and when she showed no signs of wanting his conversation, Lord Harrington began to experience a feeling of pique.

'I do so detest provincials,' said Lady Miles sympathetically, seeing Lord Harrington's attention beginning to stray in Fiona's direction. 'So naughty of Pardon to invite two such unsuitable persons to his table.'

'Mr and Miss Sinclair are from Edinburgh . . . as you are yourself,' said the earl.

'Yes, but *not* in the same circle. I am going to London for the Season. Unthinkable that one should miss it.'

'The Sinclairs are also travelling to London for the Season.'

'Indeed! How presumptuous.'

'Why is it presumption in them and not in yourself?'

'My dear Harrington. Your wits are wandering. Only look at the girl's shabby gown! You cannot compare such as I with such as Miss Sinclair.'

'No,' agreed Lord Harrington equably. 'Miss Sinclair is very beautiful.'

The covers were removed and the wreck of the mountain taken away. Decanters and bowls of fruit and nuts were put on the polished wood of the table.

'Miss Sinclair,' essayed Lord Harrington. 'May I ask your direction in London?'

To his annoyance, she turned her attention from the captain with obvious reluctance.

'Clarges Street,' said Fiona. 'Sixty-seven Clarges Street.'

'Who owns the house?'

'I do not know.'

'The Duke of Pelham has a house in Clarges Street which is said to be unlucky, and so his agent has been offering it at a very low rent. I hope that is not where you are bound.'

'In all probability, it is ... Papa being such a miser,' said Fiona, sending another brilliant smile down the table to the morose Mr Sinclair.

Mr Sinclair saw Mrs Leech rising to her feet as a sign that the ladies were to retire. He hurriedly struggled to his own. 'Thank you,' he said to Mr Pardon, 'but I fear I and my daughter must retire early. No doubt we shall be making an early start of it in the morning.'

'Nonsense, Sinclair,' said Mr Pardon with quick displeasure. 'The night is young and we are desirous of your company.'

'I fear I must insist,' said Mr Sinclair, executing a clumsy bow and heading purposefully down the table to where Fiona was sitting. He heard Mr Pardon mutter, 'Uncouth lout.'

Fiona rose gracefully at his approach, curtsied to the company, and followed him out of the dining room.

'Not a word until we get upstairs,' muttered Mr Sinclair in her ear, well aware of the listening footmen.

Once in the Yellow Room, he demanded to know how she had fared with Lord Harrington.

'Very pleasantly,' said Fiona demurely.

'He was not overwarm in his attentions, I hope?'

Fiona wrinkled her brow as if thinking hard. The clocks ticked in the silence of the room. 'No,' she said at last.

Mr Sinclair shook his heavy head and looked at her fondly. 'Poor silly wee thing,' he said. 'They must have wondered why we were so shabbily dressed, but I did not have an opportunity to explain. Ah well, I'm thinking we're best out o' company like that. It's not for the likes of us, and I was mad ever to think it. We'll just—'

'But I did,' said Fiona, spreading her hands out to the fire.

'Did what?'

'I explained why we were so shabbily dressed.'

'And what did you say?'

'I said you were a miser.'

'What!'

'I said you were a miser,' repeated Fiona patiently.

'Me! A miser! Me what's been the most open-handed man in all of Edinburgh!' Mr Sinclair clawed towards the ceiling in his rage. 'To disgrace me in front of all these fine folk.' He spluttered and cursed with fury, looking at Fiona's beautiful face with hate-filled eyes, quite forgetting he had just been on the point of taking her back to Edinburgh to protect her from the evil, sinful fleshpots of London.

Fiona sank demurely into a chair while he cursed himself dry. Then, as if he had not spoken, she looked about her and said, 'I do not like yellow.'

'You ... do ... not ... like ... yellow,' grated Mr Sinclair.

'No,' said Fiona. 'It makes me feel quite bilious.'

'The dell wi' ye,' screamed the overtired and over-wrought Mr Sinclair. 'Go into ma room and see if blue suits ye better, ye stupid widgeon. Did ever a man hae such a millstone round his neck. Awa' wi' ye and take yer traps.'

Fiona picked up her small trunk, curtsied, said, 'Good night, Papa,' and meekly went out and into the Blue Room next door.

After a few moments, Mr Sinclair came crashing in after her, collected *his* trunk, and crashed out again. All that girl was fit for was marriage fodder, he grumbled to himself as he prepared for bed. 'Pshaw!' He rammed his nightcap down on his head, turned down the oil lamp, blew out the bed candle, and climbed into the bed, which creaked and protested under his weight.

He felt uncomfortably sober. He wished he had drunk his usual fill. As the hart desireth the water brooks, so did Mr Sinclair's fatty heart long for a bumper of brandy.

He was lying, staring up at the tester, and wondering whether to ring for a servant when he suddenly fell asleep. He plunged straight down into a dream where he was attending an assembly at Almack's. He was dancing with Lady Jersey and hoping madly she would not notice he had forgotten to put on his breeches, or, for that matter, any small clothes whatsoever.

It was all very embarrassing, for Lady Jersey, a faceless figure because he did not know what she looked like, was somehow becoming very amorous. She was murmuring endearments in his ear, and then, to his horror, she seized him and kissed him passionately.

And that was how Mr Sinclair started up out of his dream to find himself wrapped in the passionate embrace of his host, Mr Pardon. He knew it was Mr Pardon because the bed candle that gentleman had brought into the room was burning brightly on a table, illuminating all the startled disgust on Mr Pardon's face.

Also the subsequent rapidly retreating voice was cursing in Mr Pardon's inimitable tones, 'A pox on all d– servants,' it was saying. 'They said the d– wench was in the d– Yellow Room.'

The door slammed. Shaken to the core, Mr Sinclair climbed out of bed, dressed hurriedly, and packed his few belongings. He roused Fiona and told her they were both going to spend the rest of the night in the kitchens 'because the bedrooms are infested with rats'.

Somehow, Mr Sinclair, who was still seething inside over Fiona having described him as a miser, did not want to tell her about Mr Pardon's attempted seduction. He was now determined to go through with the plan of taking her to London, and did not want to put her off by possibly making her think that all gentlemen were like their host. Also, he had a shrewd idea that if he accused Mr Pardon of trying to seduce his 'daughter,' then Pardon would claim he had mistaken the bedroom for that of his mistress. Moreover, all his hard-faced guests would believe him.

Fiona agreed mildly to meet him in his room as soon as she was dressed. They made their way downstairs some ten minutes later to join the rest of the passengers in the kitchens.

The coachman was relieved to see them. There had been a quick thaw, he said, and so now that Mr and Miss Sinclair had joined them, they need not wait for dawn before making their departure.

Roused from a deep sleep by the bustle outside, the Earl of Harrington drew his curtains and looked down from his bedroom window. The outside passengers were climbing onto the roof of the mail. Fiona was being helped inside the coach by Mr Sinclair. She paused with her foot on the step, looked up at the window, and smiled. He was sure she could not see him, but he caught his breath at the beauty of her face, and raised his hand in a salute.

Mr Sinclair climbed in after Fiona and slammed the door. Soon the coach was bowling down the drive through a thin curtain of driving rain.

Lord Harrington closed the curtains and turned away. He would surely never see Fiona or her father again. Despite their social ambitions and good address, it was highly unlikely that society would care to invite that shabby miser and his daughter to dine at their tables.

FOUR

Alas! how deep and painful is all payment! They hate a murderer much less than a claimant . . . Kill a man's family, and he may brook it – But keep your hands out of his breeches' pocket.

LORD BYRON, *DON JUAN*

A great wind rushed through London, tossing straw from the streets up to the rushing clouds. The new leaves on the trees in Green Park trembled and shivered. Dust whirled everywhere, making little dust devils dance at the crossings. Society ladies determined to sport their best muslins turned strange red-and-blue-mottled colours. Smoke blew down from the jumbled chimneys in long grey streams and then whipped off down the streets of the West End, depositing a gritty film of soot on curtains and clothes, carriages and horses.

Only one little thread of soot trickled down from the kitchen chimney high above Number 67 Clarges Street. For the coming of the Sinclairs had brought neither warmth nor food. Nor had it brought any invitations.

Mr Sinclair had been in London for seven whole days, and already he was considering cutting his losses and going back to Scotland, away from this alien land.

He could not join a club. He knew no one to sponsor him: in fact no one showed any signs of wanting to know him. He had endured an uncomfortable interview with the butler, Rainbird, who had asked for an increase in the wages of the staff, and he had been forced to refuse him.

When he had first arrived, he had felt everything would prosper. The house was undoubtedly a gentleman's residence. It was a typical town house of the period, tall and narrow, with three floors above a basement, each floor containing two rooms, one in the front and one in the back, with a staircase and passageway to the side. On the ground floor was a drawing room consisting of front and back parlours. On the first floor was a dining room with a bedroom at the back; on the second floor, two more bedrooms. The attic, or garret, was divided into five rooms for the servants.

He had naively supposed society would learn of their presence by a sort of osmosis and issue invitations, not knowing that matchmaking mamas arrived in London usually one whole month before the Season to 'nurse' the ground, as parliamentary candidates are said to nurse their constituents before an election.

It was all too evident that Rainbird and the rest of the staff despised the Sinclairs. Such food as was left over from the Sinclairs' meagre table would barely have fed a cat, let alone the staff of a town house.

Relations had not improved between Mr Sinclair and Fiona. He still cursed her for having described him as a miser. He had allowed her money to buy cloth to make gowns because she had said calmly she was perfectly capable of making her own. Now while he sweated and worried and keenly felt the censure of the servants, Fiona appeared totally absorbed in stitching and cutting. She did not seem to have a care in the world, which, thought Mr Sinclair sourly, all went to show the benefits of a simple brain.

Over a tough dinner of stewed mutton, his temper at last broke. 'I cannae stand yer stupid face ony mair,' he howled, his accent broadening as it always did when he was in a passion. 'Here we are, worse off than ever, barely enough to eat, and not a man in the whole of London interested enough to call.'

He put his heavy head in his plate and began to cry. 'I'm sure it's all because you said I was a miser,' he sniffed.

'As to that,' said Fiona, raising up his head and sliding a napkin under it, 'I fear Lord Harrington does not gossip. Sad to say, no one has heard you are a miser. Pity.'

Astonishment dried Mr Sinclair's tears. 'Pity? *Pity!* You daft girl!'

'If society thought you a miser and thought me your sole heir,' said Fiona, lifting up her glass of water and tilting it so that little waves ran up the side of the glass, 'and *if* they thought you had a weak heart, why, then, invitations would arrive in droves.'

'You fool,' hissed Mr Sinclair, sitting bolt upright. 'That poxy face of yours is all we have in the bank. Don't talk fustian. Don't . . .'

He stopped abruptly and stared at her while thoughts churned around in his head. First – he had not taken Fiona out walking. She had been accompanied by Joseph on her walking expeditions. Second – a reputation as a miser covered a multitude of threadbare signs of genteel poverty.

'You have a piece of mutton stuck in your ear, Papa,' said Fiona.

'Leave me,' said Mr Sinclair. 'I must *think*.'

Fiona rose gracefully to her feet. She went out quietly and stood in the shadowy hall. She took a half step back towards the dining room and then changed her mind. Rainbird entered the hall. Fiona smiled at him vaguely and then tripped lightly up the stairs, holding up the skirts of her old crimson gown.

Rainbird went in to the dining room. 'Will there be anything else?' he asked.

'No, no,' said Mr Sinclair, dabbing at the meat and gravy stuck to the side of his face. 'Bring me my port into the front parlour in, say, half an hour.'

'Very good, sir,' said Rainbird gloomily. He

made a stately exit and went down to the servants' hall.

'Wants his port in half an hour,' he said, throwing himself down at the table. 'There's only half a decanter left. Does he know that? Does he know we can barely feed *them* let alone ourselves on the housekeeping allowance? Mrs Middleton, tallow candles he wants. Tallow! No need for beeswax he said to me yesterday. Tcha!'

The staff were too cast down to answer him. Lizzie kept away from the others, sitting in a chair by the small smoky fire. It had been so wonderful just before Mr Sinclair had arrived. They had all been scrubbed and clean and shining and hopeful. Certainly their easy informality with each other had gone. They had fallen into their places in the servants' hierarchy, which was as rigid and snobbish as that of the *ton*.

But they had all been pent up and excited, dreaming of the food they would have and the vails they would get. Rainbird had even been down to the mews at the end of the street to seek out likely grooms and a coachman in case the new tenant should not bring his own.

Rainbird was remembering, too, the excitement that had preceded the Sinclairs' arrival. April first, the day when Palmer had told them Mr Sinclair would appear, Rainbird was out waiting on the step, preening himself a little under the watchful eyes of the servants in the neighbouring houses.

But the day faded into dusk, and there was still

no sign of the Sinclairs. Excitement began to fade among the staff. Rainbird ate his evening meal and then went back out again for a last look.

A dusty hack pulled by a broken-down horse rounded the corner from Piccadilly and came to a stop in front of the house. Rainbird went forward to tell the driver to go away. God forbid that Mr Sinclair should arrive and see such a disgrace of a vehicle outside his residence.

'Move on,' he called to the jehu on the box.

'Won't,' said the driver laconically. 'This is the h'address what this 'ere cove in the back wants.'

A chill feeling of dread began to grow in the pit of the butler's stomach. The carriage door opened, and a fat portly gentleman in old-fashioned clothes inched down backwards into the street. He held out his hand and helped down a female figure closely wrapped in a long hooded cloak.

The gentleman turned about and saw Rainbird. 'You,' he called. 'Fetch the imperials.'

'Mr Sinclair?' asked Rainbird faintly.

'The same.'

'Joseph!' called Rainbird. Joseph came swanning out, one hand on his hip.

'Fetch Mr Sinclair's baggage. Quickly,' added Rainbird as Joseph's mouth fell open.

Mr Sinclair paid the hack, and there was an unpleasant scene as the driver howled over the paucity of the tip.

Rainbird shook his head and came back to the present. He wearily rose to his feet. May as well look out the port. He was sorry he would not have a chance of looking at Miss Sinclair. She was a dreamy, vague girl, but so dazzlingly fair that it eased the pain at his heart. Rainbird felt the humiliation of having a poverty-stricken master keenly because he felt responsible for the other servants. Already servants from the houses on either side were making jeering, slighting remarks.

Rainbird took the half decanter of port and climbed the stairs. Good servants *never* knock. He opened the door of the parlour and then stood stock still, staring at the scene before him.

Seemingly oblivious to his presence, Mr Sinclair was counting gold coins into a brass-bound strong box. Gold glittered through the old man's fingers. 'One hundred and one thousand,' Mr Sinclair was muttering. 'One hundred and one thousand and one . . .'

Then Mr Sinclair looked up and saw the butler. He shovelled the gold back into the box – 'so much of it,' as Rainbird was to say afterwards, 'that it spilled down the sides.'

'I am a poor man,' gabbled Mr Sinclair. 'You saw nothing . . . nothing.'

'No, sir,' said Rainbird impassively, although his heart was beating hard. He set the silver tray with decanter and glass on a table and withdrew.

He erupted into the kitchen, babbling of the gold he had seen. 'Mountains of it,' he gasped. 'The man's a *miser!*'

Slowly they all turned and looked at little Lizzie,

who sat crouched in front of the fire. 'This is what comes of listening to you and your papist beliefs,' sniffed Mrs Middleton. 'You will scrub the kitchen floor until it shines and that will do you more good than candles and painted images.'

Upstairs, Mr Sinclair sadly pulled his waistcoat out of the strong box where he had stuffed it before putting his guineas on top to make it look like a miser's hoard. He only hoped Rainbird would gossip to the neighbouring servants.

It would be quite dreadful if he did not!

But it was Joseph who started the gossip, Joseph who was so bitter and put down by that Luke next door who strutted up and down in his new pink livery with the gold lace.

Luke noticed with satisfaction Joseph's envious glare and said, 'Looking's all you're going to get, my fine buck. *Your* master couldn't even afford one of my shoulder knots.'

'My master,' said Joseph passionately, 'could buy and sell yours.'

'Garn!'

''S the truth. He has a box with thousands and thousands of golden guineas. 'E's a miser, that's what 'e is.'

To Joseph's gratification, Luke's eyes grew rounder and rounder. 'Mr Blenkinsop,' called Luke to his own butler who was just emerging from Number 65. 'Come here, Mr Blenkinsop, please sir. You never did in all your born.'

Mr Blenkinsop made his stately approach and inclined his head gravely to hear the tale of misers and guineas.

'Terrible, terrible,' he said ponderously. 'Be so good, Joseph, as to step indoors and ask Mr Rainbird if he would care to join me at The Running Footman for a tankard.'

And so Rainbird joined Mr Blenkinsop, and, warmed by the fascinated interest of an appreciative audience in The Running Footman, which was the upper servants' pub, he told the tale of the miser of Mayfair. So the gossip, like a stone dropped in a pond, spread out in ripples through the ranks of the servants from Grosvenor Square to St James's Square, and the servants talked to their masters and mistresses, who talked to each other.

The next day was a day to remember. Mr Sinclair announced his intention of taking his 'daughter' for a walk in Hyde Park at the fashionable hour.

At first the cynical servants, who had been told to expect Mr Sinclair and his *ward*, were inclined to think that Fiona might be his *chère-amie*. But her vague air of innocence combined with Mr Sinclair's gruff treatment of her soon put that scandalous idea to rest.

Mr Sinclair waited in the front parlour for Fiona, who had told him that she had completed her first ensemble and planned to wear it. He hoped she would not look like a country dowd. He wished now he had pressed her to take the advice of a fashionable couturier. But he had been so disappointed at their previous lack of success that he had jumped at the idea of saving money. Also, dim-witted though she was, Fiona at least appeared to be skilled in all the arts of housewifery. Mr Sinclair had grown up in Edinburgh in the town's heyday when it was called the Athens of the North and ladies were judged on their knowledge of metaphysics rather than their gowns. He believed that dressmaking and cooking came naturally to even the most feeble-minded.

Nonetheless, he looked at her in awe when she entered. She was wearing a pink crêpe dress, high-waisted and puff-sleeved and cut low enough at the neck to show she had an excellent bosom. A Circassian straw hat with the brim pinned up at one side to show her glossy black curls and slouched down at the other gave her a dashing and sophisticated appearance. She wore long gloves of a deeper rose pink, and a bunch of pink roses ornamented the crown of her hat.

'You *dasher*,' breathed Mr Sinclair.

'Let us hope I do not scare the birds from the trees,' said Fiona primly.

They entered the park, arm in arm, at the fashionable hour.

Fiona was a sensation.

Drivers reined in their carriages while their occupants stood up to get a better look. Fiona floated gracefully at Mr Sinclair's side. It was the first fine day. Fleecy clouds puffed across the blue sky above, and everything was green and fresh after the recent rain. There was something about Fiona's beauty and innocence that made even the most hardened rake think of enchanted princesses in ivory towers.

In vain did the ladies try to point out Fiona's faults. One said she was too bold, but that was such an obvious untruth that she blushed as she said it.

To Mr Sinclair's surprise, Fiona appeared to be more awake than usual. Her grey eyes scanned the carriages with interest. It was almost as if she was looking for someone.

Mr Sinclair waited until he was sure they were the centre of attention, and then he dramatically clutched his heart and made odd gargling noises.

'Papa!' cried Fiona loudly, her Scottish voice with its lilting accent carrying clearly to the surrounding spectators. 'What's amiss?'

Mr Sinclair made several choking noises, wrenched desperately at his cravat, and to all intents and purposes collapsed in a dead faint. Gentlemen rushed to give their assistance. Fiona, now kneeling in the grass beside the fallen Mr Sinclair, looked more like a romantic heroine than ever.

'Speak to me, Papa,' she urged, and even Mr Brummell, that arbiter of fashion and renowned cynic, was to say later that her silvery voice pierced him like an arrow.

Mr Sinclair opened his eyes and said faintly, 'My heart. Alas, Fiona, you know I have not long to live. Miser that I am, I have been a bad father to you. But when I die, all my gold will be yours.'

The listening company looked as if they had been galvinized by one of the new electric machines. Eager hands tenderly lifted Mr Sinclair into the famous Lord Alvanley's carriage while Mr Brummell, Alvanley's closest friend, mopped the old man's brow with his handkerchief.

A procession followed the carriage back to Clarges Street. Apparently recovered, Mr Sinclair fulsomely thanked his rescuers and urged them indoors for cakes and wine. The distracted Rainbird did his best. The wine was thin and sour and watered. The cakes were stale, bought at half price from a local bakery. Society gamely ate and drank, saving up each evidence of miserliness to relate at the dinner tables, routs, and parties later that evening.

'We barely noticed,' said Lord Petersham later. 'We were all too busy feasting our eyes on Miss Fiona's beauty.'

Downstairs that evening Rainbird carefully put all the tips he had collected from the aristocratic guests into a pot. He had faithfully promised his fellow servants that all vails would be equally shared. Mrs Middleton and Joseph had protested, claiming that Rainbird should get the main part, then Mrs Middleton herself, then the cook, then Joseph, and so on down the line. But Rainbird said they had suffered together and they may as well benefit together.

'I don't know if they'll be any more pickings,' he said gloomily, 'so let's make this last. No wasting your share on candles, Lizzie.'

'Oh, Mr Rainbird,' said Lizzie, 'I do wish you would let me pray again.'

'Enough of that, my girl,' said Rainbird. 'Pray by your bed if you must, but there's enough work here without you running off to waste your money on candles.'

'Seems to me you're touched in your upper-works, Lizzie,' tittered Joseph, and then quailed as Rainbird rounded on him fiercely. 'Now, you leave our Lizzie alone, you jackanapes,' he growled. He smiled at Lizzie, that charming smile of his that lit up his comedian's face and usually made Lizzie want to laugh. But Lizzie adored Joseph, and his remark had cut her to the quick.

'Before that Jessamy goes a-buying scent for to anoint his useless body,' said the cook, MacGregor, 'I waud suggest we could hae a wee bit o' meat for supper tomorrow. Roast beef,' he said, his eyes gleaming. 'Roast beef and gravy and lots of potatoes and we'll give them upstairs that old bit o' venison I got cheap from the butcher 'cause he dropped it in the sawdust and I saw him do it.'

'Roast beef it is then,' said Rainbird dreamily. He loosened his cravat and put his feet up on the table. It was a sign that they were all equal in hardship again and the others took their places at the table, each sitting in the nearest chair without carefully noticing rank and precedence as they had done since Mr Sinclair's arrival.

'Give us a bit of a tune, Joseph,' said Rainbird. 'This is the best day we've had for a while.'

Joseph took out his mandolin and with a wicked side-long look at Mrs Middleton began to play the opening chords of a rather bawdy ballad, but his aim of shocking the housekeeper was defeated by MacGregor, who began to make up words, all of them ridiculous, to go along with the tune. Jenny and Alice began to giggle helplessly, and little Lizzie put her hands over her mouth to stifle a laugh in case she offended Joseph.

'Tol rol diddle dol,' carolled MacGregor happily. Then his voice trailed away, and there was a sudden shocked silence. For the door had quietly opened, and Miss Fiona Sinclair stood surveying the scene.

Miss Harriet Giles-Denton and Miss Bessie Plumtree had been enjoying their evening at Mr Pardon's town house until the name of Fiona Sinclair cropped up. Their respective parents, who had brought them to London for yet another Season, had graciously allowed both of them to attend a musicale at Mr Pardon's under the stern chaperonage of a maiden aunt of Miss Plumtree, who had been engaged for the Season by the Plumtrees and Giles-Dentons to keep a watchful eye on their daughters.

The acceptability, or lack of it, of Mr Pardon had been much discussed by both families on their arrival in London, but Mr Giles-Denton had clinched the matter by saying that Pardon was well-regarded by the *ton*. This was in fact true, because Mr Pardon's more nefarious deeds had been discreetly performed in or near his mansion on the Scottish borders. Because he entertained lavishly, he was accounted no end of a good fellow.

There was a fair sprinkling of titles in his mansion that evening. There was of course Mrs Leech, but neither Bessie nor Harriet allowed themselves to think about her because to do so might conjure up unladylike feelings.

The musicale was over and the company were strolling about or sitting chatting or striking attitudes when Harriet heard Fiona's name. It quite spoiled the attitude she had been rehearsing all day, which involved propping her chin on her plump hands and scowling out into space.

Bessie, too, had been striking an attitude when that wretched name had spoiled it all. She was wearing a Turkish turban of bright blue, fringed with gold. Her gown was white-silver lame on gauze, the gauze sleeves revealing her sharp pointed elbows. Bessie's attitude was to point one finger to the centre of her brow and look dewy-eyed, the dew in her eyes being a liberal application of belladonna.

A certain Lady Disher voiced the dreaded name. 'Who is this beautiful Fiona Sinclair everyone is raving about?' she asked languidly. 'Evidently she caused quite a sensation in the park this afternoon.'

'Oh, we met *her*,' said Harriet. 'She was travelling by the mail when it broke down or something and she and her father were invited to take dinner by Mr Pardon in his home. She is nothing out of the common way. A marked Scotch accent, very bold, and badly dressed.'

Mr Pardon, who was still smarting over the humiliation of kissing Mr Sinclair, said nothing.

'But everyone – even Brummell – says she is divine. And all that money, too!' enthused Lady Disher.

'What money?' demanded Mr Pardon sourly. 'The old man hasn't a feather to fly with.'

'But he is a miser. Is it not thrilling? A veritable miser. One of his servants, the butler, I think, came upon him counting bags and bags of gold. He has a weak heart. In fact he had an attack in the park which nigh took him off to his Maker. "I will leave all my gold to you, Fiona," he was heard to say. Of course, the gentlemen are going *wild*. Gold, more gold, and the face of an angel. *Nothing* could be more seductive. They were all – all the people who helped them home, that is – offered sour watered wine and stale cakes. "Divine," says the great Brummell. "So good for the *tailleur*."'

Everyone started to show interest in the Sinclairs, although Bessie and Harriet tried every way they could to diminish Fiona's beauty and reputation.

Lady Disher moved a little away from the nodding, gossiping heads. Mr Pardon followed her. He was suffering from a mixture of fury and humiliation. It was one thing to try to seduce a penniless girl of no particular family, but another to try to ravish an heiress. Sinclair could have taken him to court. He broke out in a light film of sweat at the thought.

'Pity me,' he said lightly. 'I did not know I had a rich heiress under my roof.'

'Why? Have you a need to marry well?' laughed Lady Disher.

'We all have a need to marry well,' said Mr Pardon, thinking bitterly of the piles of unpaid bills stuffed in the pigeon holes of his bureau.

'Then propose to her by all means! Mrs Leech is, after all, only the latest mistress on the scene. You have gracefully rid yourself of them before. Would that I were a man! I find myself at low ebb.'

'What! I thought that gambling hell of yours made a fortune.'

'Shhhh! My gambling hell, as you call it, is nothing more than a gathering of ladies who play cards. They are invited to one of my little afternoons or evenings and if they feel the urge to play, who am I to deny them?'

'Perhaps we both might profit,' said Mr Pardon slowly. 'Say you were to send Miss Fiona a card – and quickly, before she is warned against you. That way you could shake some money loose from the golden tree. She will need to ask papa for the money, and he will be incensed. I will be on hand to comfort and advise him. I will offer myself as guide and protector – after I have settled your bills with his money, of course.' He mentally added, And I had better have some splendid excuse to explain what I was doing jumping on him in the middle of the night.

'I shall call on her tomorrow,' said Lady Disher.

'But what if she is shrewd? What if she takes one look around my establishment and takes her leave? What if she brings her father?'

'You always know how to play your cards,' said Mr Pardon, fanning himself delicately with a chickenskin fan. 'She is invited to afternoon tea. Ladies only. Gossip among the cups. Little game of faro, Miss Sinclair? All respectable. *You* know how it is done. If she fails to take the bait, then I will do my best to lead her back into your web, my divine spider.'

'Is she clever?'

'I did not have much conversation with her. She was next to Harrington at dinner.'

'Harrington? That devil and woman-hater? What did he say of her?'

'Nothing. You know Harrington. Never gossips.'

'He will not interfere? Did he seem *épris* in that direction?'

'When was Harrington ever *épris*? Stern, silent misogynist . . . but she did make him laugh at one point.'

'Aha! I feel the sooner I entrap Miss Fiona the better. I shall call tomorrow, and, if I fail, I will ask your help.'

'Miss Sinclair!' said Rainbird, rising to his feet. 'What a pretty servants' hall,' said Fiona vaguely. 'Is that your dinner?'

A stale loaf and a hunk of cheese stood on the table.

'Yes, miss,' said Rainbird with some asperity. 'It's all we can afford.' He thought guiltily of the tips they had received and then comforted himself with the thought that that *had* been all they could afford since they had received the money after the shops had closed.

'I know *you*, Mr Rainbird,' said Fiona. 'Now, let me see . . . that's Alice, and that's Jenny, but who is this?' She looked down the table to where Lizzie sat at the end.

'Lizzie O'Brian,' said Lizzie, bobbing a clumsy curtsy.

Fiona gazed at Lizzie's spotted face and lank hair. 'Vegetables,' she said suddenly. 'You must eat vegetables, Lizzie. Lots and lots. They will shine your hair and clear your complexion. *Raw* vegetables.'

'Like a rabbit,' sniggered Dave, the pot boy, and was cuffed into silence by Alice.

MacGregor, who had been seething like a volcano, moved forward towards where Fiona was standing, tufts of red hair sticking out from under his white skull cap. 'Now, now,' bleated Mrs Middleton, catching hold of his sleeve.

'Vegetables is it?' demanded MacGregor passionately. 'For a wee scullery maid when us can't get a bite to eat. *Vegetables!*'

'Stow your whidds and plant 'em, for the cove of the ken can cant 'em,' jeered Joseph.

'Silence, all of you,' roared Rainbird, appalled at such insubordination. 'You should be abovestairs, miss.' He marched to the door and held it open.

'I do not mind,' said Fiona, wide-eyed. 'I know that lack of food causes sharpened tempers. You will have money for food and clothes and warmth just as soon as I can arrange it.' She went quietly from the room and closed the door behind her.

The servants looked rather shame-faced. All their wrath was directed against Mr Sinclair. They felt Fiona had done nothing to deserve such a display of bad manners.

'Do you think she meant it?' asked Lizzie timidly. 'About us getting money, I mean?'

'Naw!' said Joseph. 'I been out wiff her on her errands.' Then he shook his head as if giving his slipping accent a shake to get it back into his mouth again. 'Simple, if you esk me. Wrapped herself ehround with thet cloak of hers, covered from head to foot. Never said a word to me.'

'I am afraid Miss Fiona is somewhat naive, Lizzie,' said Mrs Middleton. 'Forget her. Tomorrow we eat beef. Let us plan the menu.'

Lizzie, who slept in a makeshift bed in the scullery, said her prayers that night. Unlike the others, she worshipped Fiona, thinking her a goddess. She began to believe everything Fiona had said about getting them money and clothes and food. She decided to forego her share of the beef and see if MacGregor would allow her some vegetables.

She rose at five in the morning as it was her duty to serve the other servants with their morning tea. There was a little package beside the scullery sink.

Lizzie could barely read, but she recognized her own name, neatly printed on the outside of the package. She put her shaking hands to her mouth, thinking the fairies had crept in during the night. At last, she crossed herself and opened the little package.

Inside lay one long cherry-red silk ribbon. Lizzie thought it was the most beautiful thing she had ever seen. There was a small slip of paper with it with only one sentence of writing. Something stopped Lizzie from asking Rainbird to read it to her. Something stopped her from telling any of the others about her present. She did not want anyone to laugh at her or possibly take the ribbon away from her.

Between her duties, she returned to the note, painfully deciphering each word until by evening she had it all. It said simply, 'To tie up your hair. F. Sinclair.'

A warm comfortable glow spread through Lizzie's thin frame. Even when MacGregor dumped a plate of raw vegetables down in front of her and gave a cackling, jeering laugh, she still continued to glow. The others ate roast beef while abovestairs Mr Sinclair and Fiona fought with a leathery and athletic piece of venison.

But Mr Sinclair was well pleased. They had had many callers including a certain Lady Disher, who had been most gracious to Fiona and had invited her to tea on the following day. 'Not *you*, Mr Sinclair,' Lady Disher had teased. 'Ladies only.'

And Mr Sinclair, flattered that Fiona's newfound friend should be a lady of quality, eagerly pressed her to accept the invitation.

FIVE

*What have I done, so very wicked, that I may not ever again
behold him? I will wait at his door, every night that I
ascertain he is from home, and, the first time he happens to
return on foot, I cannot fail to see him; and one word he must
say to me, if it is but to order me home. Something like the
man who boasted of having been addressed by the Emperor
Bonaparte; What did he say to you? somebody asked.* Va
t'en, coquin, *answered this true Christian.*

HARRIETTE WILSON'S MEMOIRS

The Earl of Harrington pulled his shirt on after a
bout in Gentleman Jackson's Boxing Saloon. John
'Gentleman' Jackson was English boxing champion
from 1795 to 1803, although such was his enormous
strength that he needed to appear in the ring only
three times.

The earl's friend, Mr Toby Masters, looked
wistfully at Harrington's powerful chest and slim
waist and then ruefully down at his own corpu-
lence. Mr Masters loved eating and drinking,
preferably to excess. He was uncomfortably aware

of the heat of the room and the itching of his skin beneath his tight corset.

'Have you heard about the latest beauty?' he asked.

'Hear of all sorts of beauties,' said the earl, shrugging his broad shoulders into his coat. 'Who is the latest fair charmer?'

'A Miss Fiona Sinclair.'

The earl stood very still, his coat half up over his shoulders. 'I have met a Miss Fiona Sinclair,' he said slowly.

'Lucky dog,' said Mr Masters. 'Have you called on her already?'

'No, not I,' said the earl, settling his coat and straightening his lapels. 'I met her when she was travelling south. She and her father were journeying by the mail that was stopped by a storm. The same storm drove me to take refuge with Pardon, who also took in the passengers from the mail. Only a storm would force me to throw myself on that creature's hospitality. He was much struck by Miss Fiona's beauty and begged her father to join the guests at his dinner table.'

'Pardon's good *ton*,' said Mr Masters.

'He raped a servant girl last year. A great scandal, ineffectively hushed up in the north. I was staying with the Chalfonts in Dumfriess when I heard about it.'

'Surely not!' exclaimed Mr Masters. 'He is too weak and foppish a fellow to be a threat to any female.'

'He was saved from prosecution only after the girl hanged herself and the father was paid a considerable sum to keep his mouth shut. But to return to Miss Fiona. She was seated beside me at dinner. An odd girl. Rather shabby.'

'Can't be the same one,' said Mr Masters. 'This one's divinely fair and dresses like a fashion plate. Father's a miser with a weak heart and plans to leave the moneybags to the daughter. They're all around her like wasps around a honeypot.'

'I shall not be of their number,' said the earl.

'Don't understand it,' said Mr Masters. 'If I had your figure, fortune, and looks, I'd be on Miss Fiona's doorstep with a proposal of marriage. Don't you like the ladies?'

'Toby, you know very well that I have enjoyed the favours of several ladies. I am not a monk. However, I do not want to marry one of them until I have decided I should produce an heir. There is not one of them that does not grow tiresome, demanding, and clinging after a time. A grand passion lasts only eighteen months, and, after that, what have you? Usually a lady with whom you have nothing in common. Passion is a cheat. I prefer to use it rather than have it use me.'

'But Miss Fiona is so very beautiful. I saw her in the park.'

'Beauty fades. Also great beauties are tiresome creatures. They are so used to their looks getting them all the attention that they have never studied how to please or amuse. *Nothing*, my dear Toby, could possibly persuade me to call on Miss Fiona. Nothing!'

* * *

'Are you sure that dress didn't cost a fortune?' asked Mr Sinclair suspiciously as Fiona drew on her gloves preparatory to leaving for Lady Disher's.

'No, I made it,' said Fiona equably.

Mr Sinclair studied her thoughtfully. Even to his untutored eye the stitching and line of her gown were exquisite. It was of fresh sprigged muslin. Over it, she was wearing a short spencer with a stand-up collar that framed her face. The brim of her straw hat was decorated with silk roses of old gold, which matched the gold sprigged embroidery of her gown.

'That's a new bonnet,' said Mr Sinclair at last.

'It is the bonnet I wore to the park,' said Fiona. 'I straightened the brim and refurbished it.'

'I'm sure I didn't give you enough money to pay for the silk for all them roses.'

'No, you didn't.' Fiona gave a delicate yawn and peered into her reticule, which was also of gold silk.

'Then where did you get it?' demanded Mr Sinclair impatiently.

A small crease marred the perfection of Fiona's brow. 'I have decided to marry the Earl of Harrington,' she said.

'You're all about in your upper chambers, girl,' snapped Mr Sinclair, forgetting the roses in his amazement. His nerves were frayed. He felt odd and alien in London. He missed Scotland and the taverns of Edinburgh. He missed soft Scottish voices and Scottish ale. He didn't like the English.

He never had, he realized. You never knew where you were with them. If a Scotchman liked you, well, he liked you for life. An Englishman was quite prepared to like you just so long as you had something he wanted – be it money, position, or title.

He took a deep breath. 'I have heard about Harrington. He's in his thirties, has never married, and is quite open about the fact he does not intend to marry until he finds a female of equal rank who will bear him stout sons. He has oft been heard saying it is shameful that men should put so much time and effort into blood lines in breeding dogs and horses and yet neglect their own nursery. He was not in the slightest interested in you at Pardon's. So he'll find himself an iron-faced aristocrat with broad child-bearing hips and a good fortune. Get some member of the gentry to fall so madly in love with you that he won't mind learning you have no money after all. And be quick about it. We had 800 guineas before we left Edinburgh, enough to have kept us in a simple way in Scotland for a goodly time. But here! Demme, they'll stake more than that on whether one goose will cross the road before the other.'

'Yes, Papa,' said Fiona demurely. 'But I would really rather have the earl.'

'Well, you can't. Why do you want him anyway? You have so far shown not the slightest interest in any man you have met.'

'I like his eyes,' said Fiona dreamily. 'He has eyes like a peregrine falcon.'

'God grant me patience!' Mr Sinclair's face softened as he looked at the beautiful bewilderment in Fiona's eyes. 'You're just a simple Edinburgh lass,' he said, 'and must be guided by me. Now, let's hear no more of Harrington. I learned all about him from some of our new friends. He's not for you. You may be lacking in wit, but you're a fine needlewoman. Did they teach you at the orphanage?'

'Oh, no. Mr Jamie hired a seamstress to teach me. And a governess.'

'That's not like him. He must ha' had something devious in mind.'

'I do not think so,' said Fiona, all pretty puzzlement. 'He said there were many ways in which I could reward him when he made a lady of me.'

'I've nae doot,' said Mr Sinclair dryly. 'Off wi' ye and take Joseph. That jackanapes is to wait at Lady Disher's and bring you home.'

Joseph was delighted to oblige. Now that Miss Sinclair was no longer muffled in a cloak, he knew they would be the centre of attention.

Mr Sinclair crossed to the window to watch them walk off down the street. A hesitant cough from the doorway made him turn round. Rainbird stood there with Jenny, the chambermaid, behind him.

'What is it?' demanded Mr Sinclair.

'A pair of gold silk curtains is missing from Miss Sinclair's bedchamber,' said Rainbird. 'I am naturally anxious that no blame is put on Jenny here.'

Mr Sinclair turned back to the window. Fiona

and Joseph had disappeared from view. He pushed past the startled Rainbird and rushed out into the street. Fiona was just turning the corner into Curzon Street with Joseph two paces behind.

'Hi!' called Mr Sinclair. 'Come back here!'

Fiona waved. Her reticule of old gold silk gleamed in the sunlight. Then she turned the corner and was gone.

Mr Sinclair stumped back indoors, sweating heavily. 'I think you will find,' he said, avoiding Rainbird's bright, intelligent stare, 'that Miss Fiona sent them out to be repaired.'

'But there was nothing up with them, sir,' said Jenny.

'Silence!' roared Mr Sinclair. 'If I say they were sent out to be repaired, then that's what happened to them.'

Startled at his rage, Jenny burst into tears while Rainbird looked at the tenant of 67 Clarges Street reproachfully.

'Well, don't hang about,' snapped Mr Sinclair. 'Time's money. *My* money.'

Rainbird led the still weeping Jenny out while Mr Sinclair sat down and cursed fluently. He now knew where Fiona had found the silk for her roses and her reticule. It was downright dishonest of the girl and would cost him money because he would need to replace the curtains. Damn her!

Was she *really* simple-minded, or had he perhaps a crook on his hands? Mr Sinclair was, however, now convinced that he had thought up the whole scheme of the miser of Mayfair by himself. He could not bring himself to think there was any cunning in Fiona at all.

Invitations had been arriving by every post. By the end of the following week, he and Fiona could start to eat at someone else's expense. But Mr Sinclair felt weighed down with guilt over the servants' predicament. He felt Palmer should pay them more and not depend on the generosity of his tenants, but that was the sad way Britain was going. Waiters in inns were expected to earn their wages out of tips, and you could not quit your room at the end of a stay without being faced with a whole line of servants who had their hands out. Mr Sinclair had been used to spending money freely. Now, he was having to guard every penny like the miser he was supposed to be.

He wanted to go out, but the idea of going out when there was no one congenial to eat or drink with seemed a miserable business. There would be callers, of course, hoping for a glimpse of Fiona. But he did not feel he could bear to sit about, watching them wince over their cheap, watered wine, seeing the thinly veiled contempt in their eyes.

He thought about Fiona again, and it struck him afresh that he really did not know the girl. He was sure Jamie had spent money on her education with a view to marrying her off profitably to one of his friends. Mayhap he wanted her for himself!

Mr Sinclair decided the time had come to sit down with Fiona on her return and try to find out what really went on behind that alabaster brow.

Down in the kitchen, Dave, the pot boy, was bowing and scraping before Lizzie. 'Good day to you, madam,' he was saying. 'You is so grand a lady, I is frit to touch the 'em o your gown.'

'Stow it,' said Rainbird, who had turned the weeping Jenny over to Mrs Middleton. 'Leave the girl alone.'

'But *look* at 'er, Mr Rainbird,' crowed Dave.

Lizzie tried to hide herself by crouching down and polishing the spit in front of the hearth.

'Stand up, Lizzie,' ordered Rainbird.

Lizzie stood up, head bowed, reddened hands twisting a knot in her coarse apron. Her lank greasy hair was now a soft shining brown and was confined at the nape of her neck with a jaunty cherry silk ribbon.

'Where did you get that ribbon, Lizzie?' demanded Rainbird.

All in that moment, Lizzie decided to lie. She knew the servants despised the Sinclairs and to say she had had a present from Miss Fiona would be tantamount to saying Napoleon Bonaparte had sent it.

'It was out in the area, Mr Rainbird, sir,' whispered Lizzie. 'It had blown against the railing.'

'Very well,' said Rainbird slowly. 'But your hair looks different.'

'I washed it under the scullery pump,' said Lizzie.

'WHAT!'

All the servants stared at her in horror.

'Lizzie, Lizzie, *Lizzie*,' said Mrs Middleton sorrowfully. 'Don't ever do anything as silly as that again. Combing the hair regularly and cleaning it from time to time with hair bran or ivory powder is quite sufficient.'

'That is true, Lizzie,' said Rainbird seriously. 'Frequent bathing of the whole body may be allowed and a little soap may even be added to the water, but washing the head is absolutely forbidden. It is a pernicious practise which brings on headache, earache, toothache, and complaints of the eyes. You see, no matter how hard you try, it is impossible to get hair really dry at the roots. This obviously keeps the brain in a constant state of humidity, and, you can see for yourself, humidity has to escape somewhere, hence watery eyes, running noses, suppurating ears, and frequent swelling of the gums.'

'How could *I* afford ivory powder?' said Lizzie. 'Miss Fiona cleans her hair by washing it regular.'

Immediately Lizzie wished she had not spoken.

'Miss Fiona,' said Rainbird in accents of deepest contempt, 'is *Scotch*, and everyone knows they are little better than savages.'

'*Whit!*' roared MacGregor, raising a meat cleaver. It took Rainbird the rest of the day to calm the angry cook down. He felt quite out of charity with Lizzie, whom he blamed for having started the whole thing. He would need to keep an eye on that young girl. She was coming over all independent and bold.

Fiona was rather relieved to find there were no gentlemen present at Lady Disher's smart house. Gentlemen did stare so.

Tea was served with delicious sandwiches and cakes. The other ladies, who had fashionably professed to have appetites like birds, watched in amazement as Miss Fiona Sinclair calmly demolished plate after plate with a seemingly unimpaired appetite.

Fiona was about the only unmarried miss there. The rest were rather fast young matrons dressed in the extremes of fashion, barely able to walk across the floor because of the tightness of their figure-hugging petticoats, that long tube considered *de rigueur* for showing the shape under a near-transparent muslin gown.

The footmen were black, something that appeared to engage Miss Sinclair's interest more than the company. 'You appear fascinated by my footmen,' remarked Lady Disher tartly, wondering whether this gorgeous beauty was ever going to stop eating.

'I have never seen anyone black before,' said Fiona. 'It appears to make them look much cleaner than white people and serves to show off the colours of their livery splendidly.'

Lady Disher blinked.

Fiona's white, graceful hand slid forward to take yet another cake. Lady Disher sensed the restlessness of their guests, and said brightly, 'Do you play cards, Miss Sinclair?'

'Oh, no,' said Fiona sweetly.

'But we all adore a hand of whist or faro. Surely you would care to join us?'

'I am sure it will all be too much for my poor brain,' said Fiona with her blinding smile. 'Perhaps it would be better if I watched. Also, I have heard that people play for money, and I have none with me.'

The ladies exchanged covert glances. Mr Sinclair must indeed be a miser. After all, had not *La Belle Assemblee* just stated in its most recent issue, 'No lady of fashion appears in public without a reticule – which contains her handkerchief, fan, essence bottle, and *card money*.' For a lady to appear at any London function without any money at all was unheard of – or had been until Miss Fiona Sinclair appeared on the scene.

'As to that,' said Lady Disher with a light laugh, 'do not worry. We will accept your vowels.'

'How very nice of you,' said Fiona. 'It is my Scotch accent, you see. I was afraid my vowels would be unacceptable. They are a trifle broad.'

A hard-faced gambler called Mrs Carrington boomed, 'Lady Disher means that if you owe anyone money, you simply write an I.O.U. – your vowels – saying you promise to pay it.'

'That is very trusting,' said Fiona, and smiled again.

'So you will play?' asked Lady Disher eagerly.

'May I take some of these delicious cakes and sandwiches home with me?' asked Fiona.

There was a shocked silence. But Lady Disher was anxious to get her hands on some of the miser of Mayfair's gold, and so she said, 'Certainly,' in a thin voice. 'Charles,' she called to a large black footman, 'go down to the kitchens and tell them to make up a basket of sandwiches and cakes for Miss Sinclair.'

As the last morsel of cake icing disappeared into Fiona's mouth, Lady Disher desperately signalled to her other footmen to clear away the tea tables. Fiona looked wistfully after all the remains of the splendid tea as everything was borne away.

Card tables were carried in, and the ladies got down to business. Gossip and chatter died. They were silent and intense, and some of them had even turned their spencers and pelisses inside out for luck.

Lady Disher sat next to Fiona to instruct her in the game. Her plan was to let Fiona win a great deal of money and then begin to fleece her.

The stakes were very high. By the end of the third game, Fiona had won £500. 'What a lot of money,' she said dizzily as a sheaf of notes and a pile of guineas were placed in front of her.

'Well, I am sure you will now feel secure enough to play with a will,' said Lady Disher. The cards were dealt. Lady Disher sat back with a calm smile on her face. She was now prepared for the kill. She rarely fleeced anyone as she now planned to fleece Fiona. The regulars present were allowed to win on some days and lose on others. They were all such addicted gamblers that they never quite realized they always lost much more than they gained.

'You seem to understand the cards very well for a beginner,' said Lady Disher.

'Thank you,' said Fiona, her voice so low it carried only to Lady Disher's sharp ears. 'At first I was confused.' Her slim fingers ran delicately over the backs of the cards. 'I see now that two pin pricks on the back means an ace, four a king, one a queen, and—'

Lady Disher snatched the cards from her. 'My servants have been playing tricks,' she hissed. She gathered up the cards from the other players. 'They are also very greasy.' She smiled. 'Perhaps we will break open a new pack.'

'Shall I go round and see if the other tables have these odd cards?' asked Fiona solicitously.

'No,' said Lady Disher, beads of sweat standing out on her brow.

'No, what?' demanded Mrs Carrington suspiciously.

'Nothing ... nothing at all,' said Lady Disher brightly, tearing off the wrapping of a new deck.

Fiona looked at her with interest, as if wondering why Lady Disher was suddenly feeling the heat, for the room was pleasantly cool. Lady Disher had a sharp-featured face and when she smiled, which was often, she revealed a row of strong, yellow teeth. But she was not smiling now. Grooves ran down either side of her mouth, and her eyes were hard and flat.

Determined to do things in the proper manner, Fiona scowled horribly as well.

The smell of a lady's perspiration was often savoured by the gentlemen who referred to it delicately as *bouquet de corsage*. But as Fiona continued to win steadily, the smell of fear emanating from Lady Disher was far from pleasant. By the time she had amassed £1,500, Fiona was beginning to feel dizzy and uncomfortable.

'I must leave,' she said suddenly. With quick, deft movements, she gathered up all the coins and notes and stuffed them into her reticule.

'You *can't!*' wailed Lady Disher, clutching at her sleeve.

'But I must,' said Fiona, arching her delicate brows in surprise. 'Papa will be lonely without me.'

Lady Disher looked wildly about her. But she had lost her allies at the other tables. They were glad to see Lady Disher get her comeuppance for once, and she had not given them a chance of getting any of the miser's gold away from Fiona. She had invited only her cronies, Mrs Carrington and Mrs Jensen, to play with Fiona. Both these ladies had considerable fortunes and often lost several thousand at a sitting without a blink.

Lady Disher could not appeal to either Mrs Carrington or Mrs Jensen for help, for neither of these friends of hers knew about the marked cards, and Lady Disher was suddenly quite sure that if she did not let Fiona leave, then, in her artless way, Fiona would tell them.

There was only one person she could turn to.

Smiling all about her, Fiona made her way out. Joseph, who had been slouched in a chair in the hall, hurriedly got to his feet.

'Goodbye, Miss Sinclair,' said Lady Disher. 'You must return soon and give us our revenge.'

'Of course,' said Fiona. 'Thank you for an exceeding pleasant and ... er ... rewarding afternoon. Oh, the sandwiches and cakes you promised me ... ?'

Lady Disher bit back the unladylike retort that had risen to her lips. 'I shall go down to the kitchens myself and make sure they are ready for you,' she grated instead.

Lady Disher slammed into the kitchens and went straight to the pantry, where she found her butler, Seamus O'Flaherty, sampling the port.

'Seamus,' she snapped, preferring to call her butler by his first name as she found the 'O'Flaherty' a bit of a mouthful. She felt anyway that servants should be like sheepdogs and have short names so that they could be the quicker called to heel.

'Seamus, a certain Miss Sinclair is on the point of leaving. She has tricked me out of a large sum of money. She is guarded only by an effeminate footman. There is a basket of cakes and sandwiches on the kitchen table for her. Follow me upstairs with the basket and then follow Miss Sinclair. Before she gets home, which is at the Piccadilly end of Clarges Street, snatch her reticule and bring it back here.'

Seamus nodded. He was a wizened little individ-
ual. But he was wiry and tough and had performed
this sort of service for Lady Disher before.

Lady Disher's house was in Manchester Square.
Joseph had expected Fiona would return the way
they had come – that is that she would cross over
Oxford Street to North Audley Street, across
Grosvenor Square, down South Audley Street, then
along Curzon Street and so into Clarges Street. To
his surprise, she turned left on Oxford Street and
started heading east.

'Excuse me, miss,' said Joseph. 'I hope you ehre
not plenning to go down New Bond Street. It ain't
the place for a lady.'

'No, Joseph,' said Fiona. 'I have a desire to see
Hanover Square.'

Joseph cursed under his breath. He wore shoes
two sizes too small in order to make his feet look
tiny and refined, but his refined feet were smarting
and pinching and aching.

Fiona's beauty began to fade in front of his
jaundiced eyes. No longer did he bask in the
gawking, admiring stares she drew. He wanted to
get home and soak his tortured feet in a basin of
mustard and water.

His powdered hair was itching. Joseph longed for
expensive hair powder instead of having to damp
his hair and then plaster it with flour from the flour
bin in the kitchen. He was six feet tall with broad
shoulders and a trim waist. He had delicate, fair

features and very round blue eyes surrounded with short, weak sandy lashes, which were his despair. As Fiona glided rapidly along and Joseph had to quicken his step to keep up with her, he began to feel more and more like an old and crippled dwarf.

Once in Hanover Square, Fiona stopped and looked about her. 'Which is the Earl of Harrington's town house, Joseph?' she asked.

'Over there, Number Nineteen,' said Joseph, who knew the address of every aristocrat in the West End. Fiona had been asked by Lady Disher over the teacups whether she, Fiona, had been to the earl's town house in Hanover Square. Fiona had shaken her head but had remembered the name of the square.

Fiona stood at the edge of the gardens in the centre of the square, under the arch of a lilac tree, and studied the house with interest. Joseph stifled a groan as he eased one tortured foot slightly from its tight shoe. Finally Fiona transferred her gaze to the glory of the lilac blossom above her head.

And that is how the Earl of Harrington saw her.

He was walking home from his club in St James's. He stood stock still, captivated by the vision, at first not recognizing Fiona, only seeing a beautiful girl standing under a lilac tree, as motionless as the still blossom above her head.

Then he recognized her, and his lip curled in a sardonic smile. So Miss Sinclair had decided to join the ranks of women who got up to every vulgar trick to bring themselves to his notice. He was about to turn away when his sharp eye saw the gnarled little figure of a man in a plain fustian coat and knee breeches sidling in Fiona's direction. He had just time to take in that the little man had the upper part of his face covered by the brim of his hat and the lower by a large muffler, when he saw the fellow move like lightning.

The man darted forward and snatched at Fiona's reticule.

Fiona held on like grim death.

Seamus, for it was he, raised his fist to strike her, but Joseph seized him by the collar. Seamus twisted about and punched Joseph on the nose. Joseph burst into tears, clutching his face and wailing. It all had taken a matter of seconds. As Seamus moved to attack Fiona again, he heard the pounding of feet and saw Lord Harrington bearing down on him.

Seamus took one scared look at the blazing yellow light of rage in Lord Harrington's eyes, at his clenched fists, and at the breadth of his shoulders and ran as hard as he could out of the square. He heard Lord Harrington pounding after him and flew into a tavern in Oxford Street, crashed through to the back premises, out into the area at the back, over a wall, and down a twisting network of alleys, only pausing for breath when he no longer heard the sound of pursuit after him.

Lord Harrington, having lost Seamus, returned almost as quickly to Hanover Square. Joseph was propped up against the railings and Fiona was ineffectually trying to staunch the flow of blood from the footman's nose with a wisp of lace hand-kerchief.

'I do not know why you ladies carry such ridiculous little things,' said Lord Harrington, producing his own handkerchief. 'It is not my handkerchief,' said Fiona, taking the serviceable one that Lord Harrington was holding out. 'It is Joseph's.'

'Ooooh, I'm dyin',' wailed Joseph.

'Come along,' said the earl sharply. 'My servants will clean you up. Stand up straight, man, and walk or I will take my boot to your backside.'

Joseph sulkily straightened up and followed Fiona and the earl.

'And you, Miss Sinclair,' said the earl, 'may have some refreshment while you wait for this milksop of a servant to be fit to accompany you home.'

'Do not be hard on Joseph,' said Fiona. 'Oh! My basket.'

The earl twisted about and saw the basket Joseph had been carrying lying under the lilac tree. It seemed easier to go back and fetch it himself rather than try to get the spineless Joseph to do it.

Once indoors, and with Joseph sobbing his way down to the kitchens, Fiona looked about her with interest. It was much larger than Number 67 Clarges Street, having rooms on either side of a magnificent staircase. In fact, it was unusually large, most of the aristocracy being still reluctant to spend much on a London home, as all their interest went on their mansions and lands in the country. Most lived in town only for the Season, with perhaps an occasional jaunt during the Little Season in September.

The earl led the way through a shadowy hall over black-and-white polished tiles and showed Fiona into a library. It was a large, gloomy, book-lined room. The walls were ornamented with some dark landscapes badly in need of cleaning. There were also some gory pictures of the hunt. In one, slavering hell-hounds were dismantling a fox, and, in another, a wild-eyed deer was being mangled about the throat by what appeared to be the same pack. Two portraits of high-nosed gentlemen in powdered wigs had been hung in the darkest corner of the room as if the gentlemen were in disgrace. Small windows at the end of the room looked out onto a weedy garden.

There was no fire in the hearth and no poker, tongs, or shovel, as they had probably been put away for the summer and wrapped in paper before being liberally rubbed with goose grease. The fire basket was made of Britannia metal, so highly burnished that it looked as if a burning coal had never sullied its brilliance.

The earl rang a bell by the fireplace, and, when his butler appeared – not a weasly man like Seamus or attractive and intelligent like Rainbird, but fat and pompous – the earl said curtly, 'Fetch Mrs Grimes.'

The butler bowed and withdrew and, in a very short time, a housekeeper appeared, crackling with starch.

'Take a seat by the door, Mrs Grimes,' commanded the earl, and, to the hovering butler, 'Fetch wine and biscuits.'

'Now we are properly chaperoned,' said the earl without a trace of humour, 'please be seated, Miss Sinclair.'

Fiona smiled vaguely and sat down.

'I am sorry I could not catch your assailant. It is unusual for a lady to be attacked in this part of town while it is still daylight,' said the earl. 'You were surely not carrying jewels or money?'

'I am carrying a great deal of money,' said Fiona. 'What nasty pictures! I would not like them in a dining room. They would put me off my food. So savage.' She looked at the painting of the tortured deer.

'May I ask what you were doing carrying a great deal of money,' asked Lord Harrington.

'I won it at cards.'

'Where?'

'Lady Disher.'

'Did no one warn you against Lady Disher? I have heard said she cheats. She marks the cards.'

Fiona looked surprised. 'Is one not supposed to mark the cards?'

'Of course not.'

'Oh. The first few games the cards were marked by little pin pricks. I pointed this out to Lady Disher who became most alarmed because she thought the servants had been playing with them. But when she ordered a new pack, I simply was at my wits' end to tell which were the aces. So I marked them myself.'

'How?' demanded the earl, fighting down an unmanly desire to giggle helplessly.

'My hands were a little bit sticky from all the cakes I had eaten so I put a little bit of stick at the top of each ace.'

'That is cheating!'

'How sad,' said Fiona.

'Are you really as naive as you appear, Miss Sinclair? Sometimes I have a feeling you know very well what you are about.'

Fiona smiled at him but said nothing.

'Miss Sinclair, what were you doing in Hanover Square? Was it in the hope of seeing me?'

Her wide grey eyes with their thick fringe of sooty lashes looked at the earl with the clear, innocent candour of a young child. 'I have no reason to seek you out,' said Fiona. 'Why should I?'

'I am used to ladies trying by every means to bring themselves to my notice, Miss Sinclair.'

'How very odd,' said Fiona, stifling a yawn. 'I do hope Joseph is not going to be overlong.'

'I am sorry you find my company fatiguing.'

The butler came in bearing a tray with cakes and biscuits and wine. Fiona accepted a glass of madeira but closed her eyes at the sight of the cakes and biscuits. 'No, no more,' she said faintly. 'I ate too many this afternoon.'

A silence fell while Fiona sipped her wine and the earl studied Fiona. The sun outside had sunk lower in the sky, and a dusty shaft of gold shone through the windows to gild Fiona's face and figure and to send prisms of light flashing from the crystal glass she held in her hand.

There was a *yielding* about her, a softness and femininity that made Lord Harrington's pulses quicken. Her skin was unbelievably pure, and each little movement she made betrayed a natural grace. Little gold silk slippers peeped out from below the flounces of her gown. He wondered what her ankles were like. He wondered . . .

He gave his mind a slap, straightened up, and asked, 'And what are your impressions of London?'

'By that, I suppose, you mean what are my impressions of society,' said Fiona. 'I do not really know. It is all so bewildering. So divorced from reality.'

'In what way?'

'The government fell in April, the slave trade was abolished, Napoleon controls most of Europe and plans to invade Britain or starve her to death, and yet none of these things seem to trouble or amaze anyone. The gentlemen lay bets on everything, and the ladies try with all their wiles to find the name of my dressmaker.'

'And all these things would be discussed in polite society in Scotland?' said the earl sarcastically.

'As to the discussions that go on in polite society in Scotland, I do not know. But even at the orphanage matters of politics and state were discussed by the staff.'

'At the . . . ?'

'Oh, I hear Joseph and now I can leave,' said Fiona, showing every evidence of relief. 'Thank you for your hospitality, my lord, and for your gallant attempt to catch the malefactor. Good day to you.'

Never before had the earl felt so furious or had he been so put down. Although he had persuaded himself any feminine interest in him was motivated solely by a desire to gain his title and his fortune, it was maddening to have this belief underlined by the beautiful Miss Sinclair, who did not seem to notice him either as a man or as a desirable fortune.

He gave her a stiff bow and pointedly turned away before she had even reached the door of the library. Fiona sailed out into Hanover Square with Joseph walking behind her, carrying the basket.

'That should fetch him,' she said.

'Beg parding, miss?' demanded Joseph.

'Nothing, Joseph,' said Fiona. 'I was merely speaking to myself.'

Which all went to show, thought Joseph nastily, just what an addle-pated, hen-witted female she was. He almost forgot about the pain in his feet as they approached Number 67. He was already rehearsing the drama of the attack to tell the other servants. To his annoyance, Fiona walked with him across the hall and started down the steps leading to the basement.

The servants had just finished their evening meal when Fiona and Joseph walked in. All got to their feet and stood looking at Fiona with sullen eyes, wondering whether she was going to irritate them again by prattling on about money.

'Joseph has a basket of cakes and sandwiches for you all,' said Fiona.

She put her reticule on the table, opened the draw-string and shook out the money. 'Now, let me see,' she said, while the servants stared and gasped. 'Ah, Mr Rainbird. Here is about two hundred pounds to buy food and coals and livery. I will take the rest to my father.'

She smiled sunnily on them all and swept out.

Rainbird was the first to spring from the stricken trance that had frozen them all. He ran to the door of the servants' hall, wrenched it open, and stumbled up the stairs after Fiona.

'Thank you, miss,' he babbled. 'Oh, *thank* you.'

'Do not sound so surprised, Mr Rainbird,' said Fiona severely. 'I told you I would find you the money.' She opened the door to the hall and disappeared through it.

Rainbird went slowly down the stairs. He hardly heard anything Joseph said, Joseph who was holding forth about the attack. As he spoke, Seamus became larger and stronger until he was quite seven feet high.

'Well, Lizzie,' said Rainbird when Joseph had finally talked himself dry. 'It seems miracles do happen. There'll be a new gown for you after this.'

'Oh, thank you,' cried Lizzie, but she looked at Joseph as she spoke and not at Rainbird.

Alice raised her well-rounded arms to pat the buttery curls under her lace cap. 'It do seem to me,' she said slowly, 'as how Miss Fiona is a most unusual lady.'

'After this, I would do anything for her,' said dark and intense Jenny fiercely. '*Anything*'.

'Oh, the dishes I will prepare for them,' sang MacGregor. 'The sauces, the jellies, the cakes.'

Mrs Middleton opened the basket and carefully began to arrange the cakes and sandwiches on plates. 'Of course, I knew she was a real lady as soon as I set eyes on her,' she said.

Dave stretched out a little hand and took a pink fondant cake ornamented with an iced cherub. 'Coo'er,' he said. 'Don't it look too pretty to eat!'

'That's enough of that,' said Rainbird, slapping his hand. 'You wait until your betters have had first choice, young man.'

They slowly resumed their places at table but this time in the correct order. They were real servants again and not an odd sort of family, bound together by poverty.

Lizzie sat at the end of the table next to Jim. She hoped the others would leave her at least one of the cherub cakes.

Upstairs Mr Sinclair was still goggling and exclaiming over the money and Fiona's tale of gambling. 'You're a downy one,' he said finally, bursting out laughing and slapping his knee. 'Lor', I'd give a monkey to see Lady Disher's face. But mark my words, she sent one of her servants after you to seize that money back. You must never go there again. D'ye hear?'

'Yes, Papa. I hear,' said Fiona meekly. 'I am very tired. Please forgive me. I must go to bed.'

It was only after she had left that Mr Sinclair remembered he had not asked her whether she had stage-managed the whole thing. Fiona was either a very lucky innocent or a very cunning young woman indeed!

SIX

The only talent I could ever discover in this beau (George Brummell) was that of having well-fashioned the character of a gentleman, and proved himself a tolerably good actor; yet, to a nice observer, a certain impenetrable, unnatural stiffness of manner proved him but nature's journeyman after all; but then his wig – his new French wig – was nature itself.

HARRIETTE WILSON'S MEMOIRS

Mr Sinclair was surprised to receive a call from the Earl of Harrington the following afternoon. Fiona had disappeared to 'a little tea party' with Mrs Carrington. Mrs Carrington had in fact called to lure Fiona to a new gaming house for ladies in St James's where Mrs Carrington was allowed free refreshments if she brought in new blood. Although she was still a very wealthy woman despite losing thousands at the tables, Mrs Carrington prided herself on her economy – which meant saving on everything other than cards.

For some reason Fiona had not told Mr Sinclair where she was going, or rather she did not give the lie to Mrs Carrington's mendacious statement that it was nothing more than a ladies' tea party.

On seeing the earl again, Mr Sinclair thought afresh that his poor Fiona had certainly no hope in that quarter. The earl looked hard and handsome and austere. He seemed almost relieved to learn that Fiona was gone from home, merely saying with chilly civility that he had come to present his compliments to the Sinclairs and make sure there had been no further assaults.

Mr Sinclair assured him there had not, and then, to the earl's extreme irritation, added with surprise, 'Gossip certainly travels fast in London. How did you come to learn of the attack on Fiona so soon?'

'I was there,' said Lord Harrington frostily. 'In fact, I pursued the assailant and subsequently entertained Miss Sinclair to refreshments in my home.'

'She didnae say a word to me,' said Mr Sinclair. 'Ah, weel, it probably slipped her wee mind.'

Not knowing Mr Sinclair became more Scottish in accent and bluff of manner when he was embarrassed or distressed, Lord Harrington began to feel that his rank and fortune were as of little consequence to Mr Sinclair as they were to his daughter. He asked Mr Sinclair many polite questions about his London experiences and began to form a picture of a lonely old man who was longing to return to Scotland as soon as possible.

The refreshments offered him were surprising in view of Mr Sinclair's reputation as a miser. The wine was of the best, and the cakes were as light as thistledown.

'Shall I see Miss Sinclair at Almack's?' he asked, rising at last to take his leave.

'I should not think she would get vouchers,' said Mr Sinclair. 'I have only just applied, but I do not know any of the patronesses of the assembly rooms and the Season has already started.'

'Perhaps I might be able to do something to help,' said the earl lightly, and then cursed himself as soon as the words were out because he was sure he had no wish to know the Sinclairs further. He was just making his way out of the door when he remembered what Fiona had said that had so tantalized him.

'What orphanage?' asked the earl abruptly.

The effect of his words on Mr Sinclair was startling. The old man clutched at his heart and turned a muddy colour.

'My dear Sinclair,' exclaimed the earl, helping him into an armchair. 'Whatever has happened?'

'Naethin,' gasped Mr Sinclair. 'My heart is weak. You had best go, my lord.'

'Let me at least ring for a servant.'

'No, no!' cried Mr Sinclair so desperately that Lord Harrington felt the old man would have a seizure if he did not take his leave.

There was a mystery about the Sinclairs, thought the earl, as he made his way out of Clarges Street and across Piccadilly to Green Park. Lord Harrington had property in East Lothian in Scotland. He decided to write to his lawyers in Edinburgh and ask them to find out all they could about a certain Mr Roderick Sinclair and his daughter, Fiona.

He was bound to find out something unsavoury about their background and discover the girl was quite unsuitable. Unsuitable for what? jeered a voice in his head. He walked more quickly as if to escape it. He was glad Fiona had been out. He was *sure* he was glad. The weather had turned brassy and hot. Most unusual in England. That must be the reason he was feeling so flat.

When Fiona returned, Mr Sinclair, who had meant to chide her for not having told him about her visit to Lord Harrington, who had meant to demand why the earl had asked about an orphanage, was completely thrown by the sight of the amount of money Fiona pulled out of her reticule.

'You'll get us both killed,' he gasped. 'You've been gambling again.'

'And so I have. And how exhausted I am,' Fiona replied, sighing. 'It's no use looking cross, Papa. I cannot help it if it is the fashion to invite me to tea and then almost *force* me to play cards. Ugh! What leathery ladies! They were quite furious with me for winning so much. I cannot understand it. The ones who were *not* playing with me lost thousands anyway.'

'Were you cheating again?'

'Oh, no,' said Fiona, opening her eyes very wide. 'Cheating is sinful.'

'There's enough here, more than enough to keep

us,' said Mr Sinclair. 'Don't play anymore. I feel it is dangerous. Look here, gambling isn't natural in women. It turns them vicious.'

'I will give Mr Rainbird some more money for the staff,' said Fiona. 'Poor things. They have so little.'

'You haven't been spoiling them?' asked Mr Sinclair.

'No. Grateful servants can be so useful.'

'You having been used to servants all your life,' sneered Mr Sinclair.

Fiona yawned and did not reply.

'Harrington was here,' said Mr Sinclair. Fiona showed no interest.

'He nearly gave me the apoplexy. He turned as he was leaving and asked, "What orphanage?"'

'And what explanation did he give for having asked such an odd question?'

'None. I was that upset. What were you saying to him, lassie?'

Fiona wrinkled her brow. 'I was merely wondering why no one in society discussed anything of importance with me – like politics or the war or anything.'

'Here! Don't start getting clever. There's nothing your *tonnish* fellow dislikes more than a clever female.'

Fiona laughed. 'You are always calling me addlepated. Stupidity does not seem to please you.'

'Never mind about me. The gentlemen consider it a fine thing in a woman. Harrington is no exception. I have heard it said he detests clever women,' said Mr Sinclair, who had heard nothing of the sort, but was sure Fiona would dim her hopes of marriage if she suddenly decided to pretend to be intelligent.

Fiona went quite still. Her eyes narrowed a fraction. Then she said, 'I feel sure you will find Lord Harrington did not say anything about an orphanage. We are both so worried about being found out that it is only natural we should sometimes hear the wrong thing.'

'Aye, but–' began Mr Sinclair.

'Have you dined?' interrupted Fiona.

'I was waiting for you.'

'Alas. I have eaten so many cakes and biscuits and sandwiches, I cannot eat any more.'

'That Highland cook has been banging the pots and sweating all day, or so Rainbird tells me. For pity's sake, try to eat something.'

'Very well,' said Fiona. 'I do not like to waste food.'

Dinner proved to be a work of art. The first course consisted of fish with oyster sauce, soup and fowls, roast beef and vegetables; the second of Ragôut à la Française, celery, game, cauliflower, macaroni, pastry, and cream; the dessert of walnuts, apples, raisins, almonds, pears, oranges, and cakes.

A waistcoat button popped from the front of Mr Sinclair's stomach and shot across the room like a bullet as he slowly digested the last bit of cake.

'You have done justice to an excellent dinner, Papa,' said Fiona. 'I hope my lack of appetite will go unnoticed.'

'That MacGregor is a genius.' Mr Sinclair sighed. 'We had best invite some people and show off his skill.'

'You will lose your reputation of being a miser. Besides, perhaps I will not marry – and what will we live on when we return to Scotland?' said Fiona.

'You will marry all right,' said Mr Sinclair. 'Our first social engagement is in a few days' time. The Bascombes' rout. Keep silly ideas about Harrington out of your cockloft and we will do very well.'

Mr Sinclair began to prose on, trying to give Fiona the benefit of his wisdom. He had culled as much gossip as he could from the callers about who was important and who was not. 'Keep clear of that Brummell,' he cautioned. 'He can be dangerous if he takes you in dislike.' His voice went on and on, and it was some time before he realized to his annoyance that Fiona had fallen fast asleep in her chair. He shook her awake and ordered her off to bed.

'And what will you do?' yawned Fiona.

'I'll take a bit of a walk in the park,' said Mr Sinclair. 'I haven't been out of the house all day.'

Fiona went up to her room and sat by the window until she heard the street door slam and saw the foreshortened figure of Mr Sinclair trudging down the street.

Then she rang the bell.

A loud yawn outside heralded the arrival of Jenny, the chambermaid. Like Fiona, the servants were all suffering from an unaccustomed surfeit of food.

'Miss?' queried Jenny, stifling another massive yawn.

'Fetch Mr Rainbird,' said Fiona. Her usually gentle voice was almost curt.

Jenny scurried off, wondering what had upset the normally placid Miss Fiona. After a few moments, Rainbird appeared in the doorway.

'Come in, Mr Rainbird,' said Fiona, 'and sit down. Close the door behind you.'

Rainbird did as he was bid and then sat down on a chair beside the empty hearth while Fiona took the one opposite. Both of them wriggled a bit on the hard, lumpy upholstery to get comfortable. The servants of Number 67 Clarges Street had, in the past, tried to augment their small income by removing the stuffing from the beds and furniture upholstery and selling it. Every chair and bed in the house now had an oddly depleted appearance.

Fiona handed Rainbird a pile of notes and coin. He took the money, but protested as he looked at the large amount he held in his hands.

'You have been more than generous, miss,' he said. 'I do not need all this.'

'You will find the money very useful,' said Fiona, looking half asleep.

'Yes, it will help to pay for new curtains,' said Rainbird with a twinkle in his eye. The servants had managed to detect where the curtains had gone.

'Yes, indeed,' said Fiona. 'And it will also serve to buy back the stuffing for the chairs and beds.'

Rainbird had the grace to blush.

'Now, Mr Rainbird,' said Fiona, leaning forward. 'Before I tell you what I really want you to do for me, I must insist that no more lavish meals be served in this house. You forget that Mr Sinclair is a miser, and I do not wish him upset by signs of overindulgence.'

'MacGregor will be in sore distress,' said Rainbird. 'He was beginning to enjoy using all his skills again.'

'Then he may practise them in the servants' hall,' said Fiona. 'I do not care what you spend on food so long as none of it appears upstairs. One course of an evening followed by fruit will be enough for Mr Sinclair and myself. Do not pamper the guests with good wine and those delicious cakes. The cheapest you can find will do for them. Why do you stay on here on such miserable wages?'

Rainbird avoided her candid gaze. He could tell her that Palmer had refused to give the girls references, but he did not want to tell her the scandal about Joseph and himself. He felt she would not understand.

'We have become used to working together,' he said, after a pause. 'We are like a family.'

She nodded, but there was something in her manner that made Rainbird feel uncomfortable. It was hard to realize it was only pretty Miss Fiona sitting in front of him. The air crackled about him as if he were trapped in the room with an outsized, dominating personality with a will of iron.

'You wish me to perform some service for you?'

asked Rainbird to divert her mind from the subject of their wages.

'Yes,' said Fiona. 'I want you to get Lord Harrington for me.'

Rainbird's normally mobile face became devoid of expression. Thoughts of Salome demanding the head of John the Baptist flitted through his brain. Then he thought he knew the reason for his own feeling of unease. Fiona was mad.

'And how would you like his lordship?' said Rainbird, determined to humour her. Trussed, boiled, drawn and quartered? he added to himself.

'I would like him at the altar as my husband.'

Rainbird said very carefully, 'You wish to *marry* the Earl of Harrington?'

'Yes.'

'Do you wish me to *kidnap* him?' Kidnapping was a word that had originally applied to the stealing of children or apprentices from their parents and masters and shipping them to the colonies. It had just lately come to mean the abduction of someone, usually for ransom.

'Oh, no!' Fiona looked shocked. 'You must make him fall in love with me.'

'And how am I to do that?' asked Rainbird gently, as if frightened that a raised voice or any evidence of surprise would cause Miss Fiona to fall down in a fit.

'By manufacturing incidents to throw us together.'

'Such as?'

'I do not know.' Fiona gave him a blinding smile. 'But I am sure you will think of something.' She stood up as a sign that the interview was over.

To Rainbird's surprise, the other servants took the matter of getting the earl for Miss Fiona very seriously. They heard him out, and then Joseph said, 'We've got to do our best, reelly we have. You've ordered my new livery. Black and gold it is. Wait till Luke sees it. What if she takes it away suppose we don't 'elp her?'

'Miss Fiona would not do anything so petty as that,' said Jenny stoutly. 'Besides, it's only natural a young lady whose father treats her like dirt should turn to an intelligent man like Mr Rainbird for help.'

'Did she like her dinner?' asked the cook, who, of all of them, proved to be the most indifferent to the plans of his young mistress.

'As to that,' said Rainbird, 'Miss Fiona said an odd thing. If I have the right of it, you are to practise your art on us, Angus. She only wants one course served for dinner and the guests are to have the worst of everything. Do you think Mr Sinclair is not a miser at all? Do you think Miss Fiona wishes her father to *appear* to be a miser?'

'It's Miss Fiona who sees we have money while Mr Sinclair turned down your request for more wages,' pointed out Alice. 'There's nothing odd about Miss Fiona wanting a bit of help with her love-life. Course, I don't see as how she'll need any help what with her face and figure.'

'But what can we do?' asked Rainbird. 'We're only servants. It's not as if we can hold a rout and invite him.'

'Perhaps we could send him a love letter supposed to have come from her,' sighed Mrs Middleton. '"My dearest heart" . . . something like that.'

'Ugh,' said Dave, turning red about the ears.

'When Joseph was attacked,' said Lizzie timidly, 'that brought Lord Harrington and Miss Fiona together. Why don't one of us attack her ourselves and let Lord Harrington save her?'

'You were *told* that washin' your hair would make the demp go into your brain,' sneered Joseph.

But Rainbird held up his hand. 'Save her from peril,' he mused. 'It might work, Lizzie. Let me think.'

'If you are going to listen to the maunderings of a scullery maid, I'm off to The Running Footman,' said Joseph.

'Know your place, young man,' said Mrs Middleton. 'Don't ever let me catch you speaking to Mr Rainbird like that, ever again.'

'Sorry,' mumbled Joseph, eyeing Rainbird nervously, but the butler was sunk deep in thought.

'I'm off unless anyone needs me,' said Joseph, but only Lizzie looked up, Lizzie who had large tears in her pansy-brown eyes.

'I hope your feelings get hurt, Mr Joseph,' said Lizzie, 'same as you've hurt mine.'

Joseph muttered something and slammed out. He began to whistle jauntily and defiantly as he went up the area steps. Luke, the neighbour's footman, was out taking the air.

'No work to do?' asked Joseph.

'Naw,' said Luke. 'They've all taken themselves off to Almack's with Lord Brampton and gone in his carridge with *his* footmen, so that's given me some time off. And about time, too.'

'Come along o' me to The Running Footman,' said Joseph expansively. Money jingled in his pocket. It was amazing how easy it was to love the world when you had money, thought Joseph. Also, Joseph, like many servants of the *ton*, was even more rigid in matters of rank and precedence than any patroness of Almack's. Luke held the rank of first footman in a noble household. He, Joseph, was the only footman. Therefore by appearing with Luke he could underline that he was a member of the upper hierarchy of servant.

'You buying?' asked Luke suspiciously.

'All you want.' Joseph grinned.

'Right ho, then,' said Luke, linking his arm through Joseph's. The two tall, powdered footmen sauntered down the street together.

It was a magic evening for Joseph. Although his tongue was loosened with drink and he bragged openly about the generosity of London's latest beauty, he did not tell of the strange request to help Miss Fiona marry the Earl of Harrington.

That piece of gossip would go round London like wildfire, and Joseph knew that the astute Rainbird would trace it back to the proper source and use his fists to bring Joseph back to a nice understanding of what happened to indiscreet footmen.

He listened sympathetically as Luke talked about the glories of the Brewers' lady's maid at Number 63. A footman hoping to attract the attention of a lady's maid – even a first footman – was flying high, but Joseph was in favour of his friend turning his attentions upward rather than downward. Joseph himself was saved from many of the pangs of love that tortured other young male servants – for servants were not allowed to marry. It was not that he was indifferent to the sight of a well-turned ankle or a roguish eye, but rather he was too effeminate, self-absorbed, and lazy to waste much time anguishing over the opposite sex. Joseph secretly considered himself on a level with Rainbird. He was unaffected by Jenny and Alice because he considered a housemaid and a chambermaid far beneath him.

After an hour and a half, Luke sighed and said he had to be getting back to prepare the dining room for a late supper. Lurching slightly, Joseph clutched at Luke's arm on the road back to Clarges Street for he had been drinking gin and hot, and, although the mixture had given him a pleasant feeling of euphoria, it also seemed to have taken the marrow out of his bones.

The heat of the day had gone and the air smelled of that London spring mixture of horse manure, bad drains, blossom, new leaves, patchouli, and wine.

'That Miss Nancy at the Brewers',' hiccupped Joseph, 'I'm sure she would be glad to walk out with you if only you asked.'

'Perraps.' Luke grinned. 'But don't clutch me so hard. You're nigh breakin' me arm.'

Joseph released him and beamed all around. He loved the world. He loved being a footman. He loved every cobble on the street.

Luke stopped outside Number 67. 'Best be off,' he said, 'or old Blenkinsop will be after me.' Luke half turned away and then stopped and gazed open-mouthed down the area steps. Alice, the house-maid, had taken off her cap and was dreamily sitting halfway down the steps, combing her long golden curls.

'Who's that?' asked Luke.

''S our Alice. You know Alice,' said Joseph crossly.

'Don't recall as I do,' said Luke. He raised his voice. 'Evening Miss Alice,' he called.

Alice put down her brush with her usual slow languorous movements. She looked up, saw Luke, and gave him a warm smile. She rose and came slowly up the stairs. 'You're Luke, a'n't you?' said Alice.

'That's right,' said Luke eagerly. 'You do 'ave pretty hair, Miss Alice.'

Alice tossed her head and a golden tress flapped across Luke's face. Luke took the tress, wound it around one finger, and smiled down into Alice's eyes.

123

Joseph stood appalled. He felt he had never seen such an outrageous sight. Had not Luke mourned with him only the year before over the sad case of Lord Chumley's first footman who had made a cake of himself over falling in love with a housemaid? God put us in our appointed stations and anyone who tried to change the rigid hierarchy abovestairs or belowstairs was doomed to hell. Joseph was deeply shocked. He slumped off downstairs, the bland glow of gin evaporating to be replaced by a mean resentment against the whole world. As he entered the servant's hall, the first person he saw was Lizzie.

'Well, madam,' he said, lurching forward, 'you wished me ill and that's what happened, you little slut.'

Rainbird and MacGregor moved as one man.

Outside, Luke listened bemused to Alice's slow voice and neither of them paid any attention to the howls of agony that soared up from below as Joseph had his head held under the scullery pump by the cook and the butler.

While Fiona continued to enrich herself in the houses of every rapacious female gambler in London, the Earl of Harrington passed the days before the Bascombe rout by trying not to think of Miss Fiona Sinclair. He had heard she was to attend the rout. Who had not? He persuaded himself that it was only idle curiousity that had caused him to send a request for information on the Sinclairs by the mail coach. But he could not help thinking he would probably have some intelligence in a week's time since the Royal Mail only took a little more than forty-five hours to reach Edinburgh.

But when he finally dressed himself to go to the Bascombes' rout at their mansion in Green Street he had to confess to himself that he *was* looking forward to seeing the unusual Miss Sinclair again. Any woman who was aware of what was going on in this country as well as abroad was out of the common way. But he was, nonetheless, confident that a further meeting with her would prove her to be as vapid and uninteresting as any other society female. He finished dressing just as his friend, Mr Toby Masters, strolled in.

'Fine as a peacock.' Mr Masters grinned, taking in all the glory of his lordship's corbeau-coloured coat, silk knee breeches, clocked stockings, and diamond-buckled shoes. 'Is this in honour of Miss Sinclair?'

'Miss Sinclair is so vague and dreamy I doubt if she would notice if I appeared in the buff,' said the earl. 'I rescued her from deadly peril, you know.'

'When was this?'

'A few nights ago. She was standing in Hanover Square pretending to be a statue when a little rat of a man tried to snatch her reticule. I gave her wine and comfort.'

'Lucky dog. You have stolen a match on all of us.'

'Not in the slightest. Miss Fiona yawned in my face.'

'A rare pearl! I met two of the oddest females at the Cunninghams t'other night – Miss Plumtree and Miss Giles-Denton. They said they knew you intimately.'

'They were both at that dinner party of Pardon's. Friday-faced chits both of 'em.'

'You are too severe. Miss Plumtree was quite pleasant. A man of my girth and looks must of necessity find beauty among the lowliest flowers.'

'You are a well set up and likeable fellow,' said the earl, 'and that should commend you to any lady of wit and discernment.'

'Perhaps Miss Fiona will prove to be such a one.'

'Perhaps. Although I think she is asleep most of the time.'

'She is playing in deep waters, I have heard,' said Mr Masters, watching with a pang of envy as the earl bent with one fluid athletic movement to brush a piece of lint from his silk stocking. 'Seems she's been fleecing the fleecers in the ladies' gaming hells.'

'She had been to Lady Disher's, I believe,' said the earl, forbearing to mention that the fair Fiona had been cheating at cards. He reminded himself he had no reason to be discreet. Toby did not gossip to anyone other than himself. But he had a feeling of loyalty towards Fiona, a loyalty that irritated him because he did not know why he should be so careful of her reputation with this, his closest friend. 'In fact,' went on the earl, 'I believe her mysterious assailant to have been one of Disher's servants.' He leaned forward and studied the intricate pleats of his cravat in the mirror.

'Come along, then,' said Mr Masters impatiently. 'You may introduce me to this fair charmer.'

The town house of Lord and Lady Bascombe was ablaze with lights as they approached it through the smoky blue dusk.

The two men had elected to walk the short distance to Green Street from Hanover Square. Outside the Bascombes' mansion, coachmen cursed and shouted as they fought for places. Lights blazed from every window of the house, the curtains being drawn back as was the custom when a rout was held.

This rout, like all routs, was a hell of pushing and shoving on the crowded staircase to get to the rooms above. It was the fashion to invite many more guests than the house could comfortably hold. A rout was not a rout unless at least a dozen ladies fainted in the crush.

Both the earl and Mr Masters held firmly on to their hats, gloves, and canes, planning to deposit them behind some curtain on the first floor, long experience of routs having taught them that gentlemen were apt to help themselves to your accessories on the road out if they looked more expensive than their own.

In fact the whole of two-faced society paid only lip service to the ten commandments and committed adultery, stole, and cheated at cards, because, after all, it was only the eleventh commandment that mattered – Thou Shalt Not Get Found Out. Being found out was a heinous sin. Any lady or gentleman of breeding should know how to be discreet.

Mr Masters did not need to ask the earl to point out Miss Sinclair. The radiant beauty being monopolized by Mr George Brummell could be none other than she. Even the earl, who had thought himself inured to her good looks, caught his breath.

Her glossy black hair was dressed in one of the latest Grecian styles and worn without ornament. Her deceptively simple gown of green crêpe was moulded to her figure, the neck and sleeves edged with thin bands of old gold silk made from the last scraps of the bedroom curtains. Her gloves were new, being of white kid, wrinkled up to the elbow in the correct manner. Also new was the pierced and carved ivory fan she carried. The sticks and guards were in the rococo style. The double-painted paper leaf of the fan was burnished to give it a sheen – a style found only on French fans. In all, a most expensive trifle, thought the earl, and then wondered if some man had given it to her.

'Brummell is a pest,' muttered Mr Masters. 'It's always the young ones he goes after. The Prince of Wales won't court 'em unless they're old enough to be his grandmother, and Brummell will not look at any female turned twenty.'

The celebrated Beau Brummell was hailed as a very handsome man, but he was, in fact, merely pleasing in quite an ordinary way. His skin was very fair, and he had fine, light brown hair, curled and pomaded. His nose was flat, and had been flat for several years since a horse had kicked it. His figure was slim and his dress exquisite. He was an advocate of 'very fine linen, plenty of it, and country washing,' and he had done much to rid the air of ballrooms and routs of their heavy smells caused by last month's underwear and last year's bath.

Fiona was not saying anything to the beau, merely smiling sweetly and listening to everything he said with flattering interest.

'How do we get rid of him?' mumbled Mr Masters.

'Easily,' said Lord Harrington.

He walked forward and clapped the beau on the shoulder. 'Lord Amber is making his noisy way up the staircase,' said the earl. 'Wants to see you, George. He won £500 from you t'other night at Brooks's and he is clutching a sheaf of your vowels to his chest.'

Mr Brummell raised his eyebrows, which were plucked into a thin line. 'Your servant, Miss Sinclair,' he murmured.

He backed away with a slow, gliding movement – very odd – that made it look as if he were not moving at all, although he had disappeared into the throng in a matter of seconds.

'Miss Sinclair, may I present Mr Masters,' said the earl. 'Mr Masters, Miss Sinclair.'

Mr Masters had very large blue eyes. They grew wider and wider as he stared open-mouthed at

Fiona. Mr Sinclair was standing a few paces behind Fiona, glaring mulishly at the floor while Mr Pardon whispered in his ear. Lord Harrington found himself becoming irritated with his friend's stunned admiration, with his very presence – in fact, with everyone in the room.

Fiona was of medium height, but Lord Harrington was just over six feet tall. The press of guests at his back thrust the earl towards Fiona. The nearness of her body and the way she looked up into his eyes unnerved him.

'What do you think of our famous George Brummell?' asked the earl. 'Do you find his wit devastating?'

'I do not find him very witty,' said Fiona. 'He has a certain quaint dry humour which makes what he says sound like wit, but very little of what he says bears repetition. Like some very light wines, it does not travel well. I fear him. I sense that underneath he is cold and hard and satirical.'

Mr Sinclair, who had been standing a few paces behind Fiona and had just shaken off Mr Pardon, came up behind Fiona just as she made this speech. The earl smiled and bowed. 'My compliments on the beauty of your appearance, Miss Sinclair,' he said. 'Excuse me.' He bowed again and left, towing the dazed Mr Masters after him.

'What on earth did you say all that about Beau Brummell for?' hissed Mr Sinclair. 'I told you cleverness would give Harrington a disgust of you. Besides, I ain't been in London very long, but one of the first things I learned was that it don't do to criticize Brummell.'

Fiona turned and looked at him, her grey eyes completely devoid of expression. Then other courtiers crowded around, and she turned back to speak to them.

For the next half hour Mr Sinclair could find no fault with Fiona. She laughed, she talked of fans and fashions, she flattered with her eyes and enchanted with the grace of her body. Mr Sinclair rubbed his hands. Gentlemen would soon be calling on him to beg Fiona's hand in marriage.

Then Mr Sinclair saw a familiar face. An old man had arrived. He was wearing an old-fashioned powdered wig and a gold-and-green-striped evening coat that belonged to a day of gaudier fashions. 'Sir Andrew Strathkeith,' exclaimed Mr Sinclair. He had met Sir Andrew at the Edinburgh High Court some ten years ago when Sir Andrew had been a spectator at a robbery case in which Mr Sinclair had successfully defended the robber.

They had repaired to the nearest tavern for a bottle of claret and had parted after a happy boozy hour exchanging vows of friendship. But somehow Mr Sinclair had never heard further from Sir Andrew and had not had the social courage to try to seek the knight out. Even now, although he was ostensibly of the same rank and privilege as these other guests, Mr Sinclair felt shy at approaching Sir Andrew. He looked across the room at him with a sort of longing.

Then Sir Andrew saw Mr Sinclair, and his old wrinkled face lit up. He waved his arm, and Mr Sinclair happily lumbered across the room, totally unaware that Mr Pardon had just accosted Fiona.

'I was just renewing my acquaintance with your father,' said Mr Pardon.

'Your fondness for my father is very gratifying.' Fiona smiled. 'In fact, your demonstrations of affection towards him were quite overpowering.'

Mr Pardon flushed angrily. 'I mistook the room.'

Fiona gave him a stupid look. 'What room?'

'I thought it was Mrs Leech's room.'

Fiona looked bewildered. 'I seem to have missed part of your conversation, Mr Pardon. You tell me you thought it was Mrs Leech's room, but I thought we were talking about your affection for my father. What *do* you mean?'

The other men about Fiona looked amused as the normally poised and polished Mr Pardon blushed and stammered.

'I will explain some other time,' said Mr Pardon. He bowed and left. Fiona's ripple of laughter followed him across the room.

Bitch, bitch, *bitch*, thought Mr Pardon. She *dares* to make a fool of me. Well, she will find me no mean adversary. She has fleeced the gambling ladies of London. All I need to do is stir them up a bit. And then let's see what becomes of *you*, Miss Fiona Sinclair!

SEVEN

*Why, you are pursing your brows, biting your lips, and
lifting up your foot as if you would stamp it into the earth. I
must say anger becomes you; you would make a charming
Hotspur. Your everyday dining-out face is rather insipid: but
I assure you my heart is in danger when you are in the
heroics.*

THOMAS LOVE PEACOCK, *CROTCHET CASTLE*

'Why did you drag me away?' said the normally
sunny Mr Masters crossly. 'By George, she summed
up Brummell very well and before we had even
started a conversation, you took your leave.'

'Then go back by all means,' said Lord Harrington. 'I was a trifle rude, I admit. But I suddenly felt
I could not bear to waste time playing courtier to
yet another beauty at yet another rout.'

Mr Masters looked at his friend strangely. 'Well,
I think it deuced odd of you to display such a heavy
touch. For all you don't rate the beauties very high,
one would never usually know it to see you charm
'em. *I* am going back. It's enough just to be allowed
to look at her.'

Lord Harrington watched him go and turned to speak to some of his other friends. He talked of this and that while all the time he was cursing himself for his rude behaviour. Fiona Sinclair affected him very strongly. When she had criticized Brummell, his first reaction had been irritation that she should so calmly dismiss London's leading star, she who was a rank outsider. And Lord Harrington was sure she *was* an outsider despite her beauty and the modishness of her manners. There was something *foreign* about Fiona Sinclair, something that was oddly threatening to his caste, his way of life, his peace of mind.

The father must have married late in life, he mused. But what had all that been about an orphanage? Perhaps Miss Sinclair had merely been involved in some charity.

The glittering crowd shifted and moved and shifted again, and all at once Fiona was not there. A moment before, she had been in the centre of the room, surrounded by a group of admiring men, and the next, she was gone. She had probably gone downstairs to the ante room, which had been set aside for the ladies, to pin her hair or straighten her gown.

It struck him that if he went down to the hall, he might catch her as she came out and have a few words in private to make up for his lapse of manners. He would not admit to himself that one of the main reasons he had walked away from her was because he could not bear to share her company even with Toby.

People were still arriving. As he edged his way down, he saw the top of Fiona's black curls as she made her way out of the front door to the street.

What on earth was the girl about, to leave without her father or a servant? It was well known that the miser of Mayfair did not keep a carriage.

Moving quickly past the people who were still pushing their way upstairs, he gained the doorway and went out onto the steps, and stood looking to the left and right, until he saw her slim figure turn the corner of Green Street and disappear into Park Lane.

Joseph had screamed in protest against the whole idea. But now, as he checked the time on the watch Mr Rainbird had lent him, he felt a thrill of excitement. The costume had a lot to do with it.

He was dressed in a long black cloak, its hood shadowing his masked face. Anyone seeing him would take him for a young blood on his way to a ridotto.

The plan was this. Fiona would slip away from the rout at nine o' clock precisely and go into Park Lane. Joseph was to swoop down on her and appear to club her. When she pretended to scream and swoon, Rainbird was to come running up and 'rescue' Miss Fiona. He would then carry her 'unconscious' body in his arms back to the Bascombes' and make sure Lord Harrington heard of the 'brutal' attack on Fiona. Joseph was to make his escape into Hyde Park where Dave and Angus

MacGregor would be standing by to divert any pursuit.

Lord Harrington was expected to have all sorts of feelings of knight errantry roused in his chilly breast. Fiona had thought the plan a very poor one, but at last had said it would do as a sort of rehearsal until Rainbird could think of something better.

The first thing to go wrong, although Joseph did not know it, was that Rainbird had forgotten that the watch he had lent Joseph was the only timepiece at Number 67 that told the correct time. It was, therefore, a full ten minutes late when he set out followed by MacGregor and Dave.

Meanwhile, Fiona had noticed to her satisfaction that Park Lane was as quiet as they had expected it to be at that hour, most of the rich and their servants being indoors. She smiled to herself as Joseph moved out from under the shadow of a large plane tree.

'Hold hard, pretty maiden,' he cried. 'I wouldst have thy jewels.'

'Oh, *Joseph*,' hissed Fiona, exasperated. 'Do get on with it. This is not the Haymarket.'

Joseph's eyes behind the slits of his mask looked hurt. 'Then if you will not give me your jewels, I will take your life,' he shouted. He drew MacGregor's prize carving knife from under the folds of his cloak and held it up where the flickering light of the parish lamp shone on its wicked edge.

'You're supposed to *stun* me,' said Fiona. 'Not knife me. Was ever a woman so plagued–'

'Hey!'

She broke off as a shout resounded down the street. Joseph saw the figure of a man hurtling towards him and dropped the knife with a squeak of terror. He tried to make his escape but the long cloak wound itself about his legs and he stretched his length on the road.

Lord Harrington was about to pounce on him. The earl had hardly been able to believe his eyes when he had seen a tall masked figure brandishing a knife in front of Fiona.

But before he could reach Fiona's fallen assailant, she had thrown herself on him and wound her arms about his neck. She had a powerful grip and he struggled to disengage his arms.

'Let me be, Miss Sinclair,' he gasped. 'I must catch that man.'

Out of the corner of her eye, Fiona saw Joseph struggle to his feet and glimpsed the figures of Rainbird, MacGregor, and Dave hurrying along on the other side at the edge of the park.

'My hero!' said Fiona, ruthlessly tightening her grip.

The earl looked down at her with a flash of suspicion in his eyes. Fiona pulled his head down and kissed him warmly.

And that was when the Earl of Harrington forgot about assailants and daggers and routs and anything else in the whole wide world but the reeling sensations caused by the warm, clinging softness of her mouth. Her breasts were crushed against his chest, her legs against his legs. She smelled of soap and rose water.

He returned her kiss with blind, single-minded intensity, feeling himself lost and drowning and not ever wanting to rise to the surface of reality again.

When she finally, gently, freed her mouth and he twisted around, it was to find that her assailant had got clean away. It was as if he had dreamt the whole thing. Park Lane was deserted. A warm breeze stirred the leaves of the plane tree. There was a smell of dust mixed with the smell of whale oil from the parish lamp. He stared down at Fiona. She was still clasped in his arms, but her eyes were down-cast and he felt her body tremble.

'You must forgive my wanton behaviour, my lord,' said Fiona in a husky voice. 'My nerves were quite over-set.'

He put her gently away from him. 'We will pretend it never happened,' he said. 'But tell me about the attack. It was like a stage play. For one brief moment I thought I was watching some sort of charade.'

'No,' said Fiona, achieving a realistic shiver. 'It was real enough. He said he would kill me.'

'We had best return quickly to the Bascombes' and have the servants sent out to see if they can find the fellow, although I do not think there is much hope now.'

'I do not want to go back,' said Fiona in a low voice. 'I want to go home.'

'But your father . . . ?'

'Leave my father be,' said Fiona in a tired voice. 'If you do not wish to escort me home . . .'

'But of course! I consider myself honoured. My carriage will be—'

'I would rather walk.'

'Very well,' he said, looking at her curiously. 'I gather you do not want to go back to the Bascombes' even to let me get my hat and gloves?'

'No.'

'But you have no shawl, no wrap.'

'The night is very warm.'

He drew her arm through his own and walked with her down Park Lane, studying her averted face, his mind racing. It was a dreadful thought, but it was almost as if she had thrown herself at him to stop him from catching her assailant. Perhaps he had been some rejected Scottish lover.

'Who gave you that fan?' he asked. It was not what he had meant to say to her but it was the first thing that came out of his mouth.

'I bought it, my lord.'

'Ah, then I have no reason to feel jealous. I was sure an admirer sent it to you.'

'It was very expensive,' said Fiona. 'I do not think I would accept such an expensive gift from anyone.'

'You must have received many tokens of love.'

Fiona smiled but did not reply.

'But you must be used to that,' he went on. 'Everyone is stunned by your beauty.'

'Strange to be considered beautiful,' said Fiona, half to herself, 'after having thought I was ugly.

Every morning I look in my glass expecting to see another face, another woman, but it is always just me. The same.'

'Where did you come by this mad idea that you are ugly? The orphanage?'

He felt her stiffen and then she said lightly, 'I told you about the orphanage, did I not?'

'Only about some intellectual orphanage where they discussed the affairs of state. Did you do charitable work there?'

'Yes.' Fiona smiled. 'But we must not talk of deep matters. We must talk of silly things. I am told that is what you prefer.'

'You were misinformed.'

'What do you look for in a lady?'

Her question reminded him sharply of the feel and taste of her lips. What man could desire more than that?

How quiet the streets were! Only one carriage drawn by a pair of matched bays clopped along Park Lane, and from one of the houses came the faint tinkling strains of a waltz. The air was sweet and warm.

He could not kiss her again, not unless he proposed marriage to her, and he could not do that. His name belonged not only to himself but to a long line of Harringtons, and he could not lightly stain it all through raging passion for this odd girl who, he was quite sure, had a closet simply rattling with skeletons.

'You have not answered my question, my lord.'

Her voice with its enchanting Scottish lilt was low and teasing with a breaking husky note in it. He was aware of the softness of her arm against the broadcloth of his sleeve and of the way her bosom rose and fell.

They came under the light of another lamp at the corner of Piccadilly and Park Lane, and he stopped and turned her to face him, standing still and looking down at her.

Her lips looked slightly swollen, and her eyes were very large and dark. He would kiss her one more time to prove to himself that his senses had been cheating him. Just one more time.

She came trustingly into his arms as if she belonged there. His dark, hawklike face loomed over her, blotting out the light. And then his mouth descended on hers. This time it was worse . . . or better.

Now he knew what the poets meant. Now he knew what it was like to lose his very soul. He kissed her ferociously, groaning against her mouth, kissing her dizzy, kissing her breathless, kissing her until he felt he would die from frustration.

'Fiona,' he said raggedly. 'Oh, Fiona, this will not do. I must not ruin your reputation, and it will surely be ruined if someone should see us. Let me take you home.'

She walked on in silence. He could feel her retreating from him, retreating behind that calm front she presented to the world.

'I-I should not have done that,' he stammered,

and felt he was making matters worse. Although he had never before felt such scorching passion, he knew enough about it to understand it had a habit of burning out and leaving a man stranded on the bleak shores of marriage, facing a woman across the breakfast table who was nothing more than a boring stranger.

'You should not have *said* that,' said Fiona severely. 'You have neither grace nor manners.'

'I apologize,' he said stiffly. 'I was overset by the circumstances.'

'Worse and worse,' mocked Fiona. 'Go, my lord, to the courtesans like Harriette Wilson. Go and buy love without responsibility. Perhaps it is all you are fit for.'

'Madam, I admit I behaved disgracefully,' he raged. 'There is no need to taunt me.'

'Perhaps you should be taunted more often, my lord. At least it turns you into the appearance of a man of blood and sinew rather than ... a tailor's dummy.'

'God, that I had never met you, you witch.'

'You need not see me again,' pointed out Fiona with that same maddening calm. 'Go away and find some lady with a long pedigree and a long nose and a mind as pedestrian as your own.'

'Thank you,' he shouted. 'I will!'

'You may take yourself off,' said Fiona. 'Oh, what fortune! Mr Rainbird.'

The much-flustered butler had sent Joseph home with Dave and the enraged MacGregor, who was bemoaning the loss of his best knife. He had discreetly followed the couple, keeping always to the shadows on the park side of the road. They had turned into Piccadilly when he had heard their raised voices and had decided the time had come to intervene.

'I shall leave you, Miss Sinclair,' said Lord Harrington, 'and return to the Bascombes'.'

'Ah, yes,' said Fiona. 'What is more important in life than to recover one's hat and stick? Tell my father I was overcome by the heat, if you please, my lord. Do not tell him I was attacked again. His heart is bad.'

'As bad as his daughter's?' snapped the earl, receiving a fulminating glare from Rainbird. He turned on his heel and walked away.

'Oh, miss,' said Rainbird. 'I am so sorry. I was late arriving and Joseph said Lord Harrington nearly caught him, and he had the vapours in the Park and would not calm down until MacGregor threatened to throw him into the Serpentine.'

'You all did very well, Mr Rainbird,' said Fiona sadly. 'I mismanaged the whole thing. I have behaved like a wanton and given Lord Harrington a disgust of me.'

'Miss Sinclair,' said Rainbird, not looking at her, 'I saw you and his lordship a little while back, and he certainly did not look like a disgusted man.'

'Ah, Mr Rainbird,' sighed Fiona. 'No, don't walk behind me. I must talk. I must talk to someone, or I will go mad. So I will talk to you, my Rainbird, and you will forget whatever I say to you and never refer to it again.'

'Yes, miss,' said Rainbird, looking at her curiously.

'I am not Mr Sinclair's daughter. I was his brother's ward. Jamie Sinclair, the brother, was a sort of religious lecher. He took me from the orphanage and schooled me to be a lady. Although he was always correct, I sensed he could barely keep his hands off me, even when I was thirteen. I knew he wanted me for his wife. I was determined to stay with him for just as long as I could bear it. Fear of poverty made me bear it. Fear of being nameless again. Fear of cold and hunger. *You* know, Mr Rainbird.'

'Oh, miss,' said Rainbird sadly. 'I know.'

'When Mr Jamie died and I was left to the protection of Mr Sinclair, I did not mind. Mr Sinclair is kind. He has no money. He is not a miser. We planned that to explain our lack of wealth and so that I should have as many suitors to choose from as possible.

'But on the road south, we were forced by a storm to seek hospitality at a house where Lord Harrington was also a stormbound guest. He was the first man who ever told me that I was a beauty whom I believed. Mr Jamie had told me so many times I was ugly that I believed him. But Lord Harrington said it in such a cold, matter-of-fact way I was able to understand it at last. Also, his eyes did not stray from my face. He did not assault my body with his eyes the way men do. I wanted him, but I was still not sure.

'I guessed our host, Mr Pardon, planned to attack me during the night because he considered me far beneath him in social station and was therefore sure I would cause no problems. I changed rooms with Mr Sinclair. It amuses me to make people think I am vague and stupid. Mr Sinclair believed me when I told him I did not like the colour of the bedchamber.

'I waited with a glass against the wall so that I could hear what was going on in the next room. Mr Pardon came into Mr Sinclair's room and leapt on the bed, thinking I was in it.

'I thought I would rather die than have to marry some man like that with hot hands and hot eyes and hot breath. I decided I must have Lord Harrington.

'I dreamed about him for so long I persuaded myself that so fine and noble a man would not blame me for my poor background were his affections truly attached.

'But he is like all the rest,' said Fiona, striking her breast. 'I dropped a hint about the orphanage, hoping he would go out of his way to find out about me, dreaming that he would come and tell me it would not matter.

'Oh, Mr Rainbird, I am so young and silly. *I!* I, who thought myself old and clever. Oh, Mr Rainbird, my heart is *breaking!*'

Ugly sobs tore at her, and Rainbird caught her and turned her about and held her to him, rocking her against his breast and saying, 'Shhh, Miss Fiona. There, there. Please do not cry. Rainbird will take care of you.'

Poor Rainbird was shattered. The cool and beautiful Miss Sinclair had disintegrated into a sobbing lost child. His heart was wrung with pity.

Fiona at last hiccupped and dried her eyes. 'I should have been a servant and worked for you, Mr Rainbird,' she said.

'No, miss,' said Rainbird seriously, 'that would not do. Servants may not marry or they lose their jobs. You love Lord Harrington and I am sure he loves you. Who would not?'

'Lord Harrington has humiliated me,' said Fiona in a stifled voice. 'To kiss me so, and not a word of love. I will never forgive him. *Never!*'

'If only I could help,' said Rainbird wretchedly, his mobile comedian's face turning into a sad clown's face.

'Ah, Mr Rainbird, my outburst is over,' said Fiona. 'Let us put on our masks again. We are home.'

'Yes, miss. I will never speak of this to a soul, Miss Fiona. Do you wish us to continue with our plans?'

'No, Mr Rainbird. I will marry the first respectable man who asks me.'

'Wait a bit, miss. Just a little. The Season is only begun.'

'Perhaps.'

Rainbird went slowly down to the servants' hall

and ordered Jenny to take a hot posset up to Miss Fiona as the poor lady had the headache.

'I hope she is not furious with us for being late,' said MacGregor anxiously.

'No,' said Rainbird. 'She is very pleased with us all.'

'Oooh, Mr Rainbird, you looks as if you are about to cry,' said Lizzie.

Rainbird forced a smile. 'No, Lizzie. I have the headache, too. It must be the heat.'

But Rainbird had the heartache. He felt like the father of a large and needy family. So many to love and care for, and now Miss Fiona added to them.

'If Miss Fiona wants Lord Harrington,' said Rainbird, loudly and fiercely and striking the table with his fist, 'then, By George, she'll have him, if I have to tie his lordship hand and foot!'

EIGHT

It was exceeding unfortunate, in view of the sad events of the following two weeks, that Lord Harrington was gone from town and Sir Edward Kirby was not.

Sir Edward Kirby's appearance on the scene was the result of a plot to ruin Fiona by the ladies of society. Not that any of them, with the exception of Lady Disher, ever put it into words, but the general consensus was that such as Fiona Sinclair deserved to be ruined.

Gambling hostesses felt their losses keenly. Unlike the respectable gentlemen's clubs, their establishments were geared to fleecing and winning. But Fiona seemed to side-step all their machinations and become richer by the day.

Matchmaking mamas were furious because all the eligible gentlemen could not see past the glare of Fiona's beauty to their own daughters lurking in the shadow of it. The expense of a Season was such that few could contemplate putting their daughters on the Marriage Market for yet another year.

Lord Harrington had written to the powerful patronesses of Almack's before his departure, recommending they send vouchers to Miss Sinclair, but such was the general female enmity towards the girl that even those stern social rulers dared not allow her to cross the threshold of their famous assembly rooms in King Street.

It was Mr Pardon who suggested to Lady Disher that Sir Edward Kirby might be interested in ruining Fiona for a certain sum.

Sir Edward Kirby had recently returned from abroad. He was a man of great charm, an inveterate gambler, and he had the morals of a tom cat. Many were the debutantes he was rumoured to have ruined, as his taste in women ran to young virgins. Any time he looked like being called to book for his crimes, he simply left the country.

Like all womanizers, he appeared genuinely to like women. Even girls warned against him fell like ninepins before his charm. He was not particularly good-looking, being only of average height and with rather thin hair, but he had a merry boyish countenance and twinkling blue eyes. He never seemed to age, and his charm of manner and dexterity in seduction improved with the years.

Although he enjoyed all the luxuries of life, like most hardened gamblers he was often plagued by duns.

Mr Pardon invited him to dinner with Lady Disher and three of the other gambling-hell owners whom Fiona had made poorer. No one was quite so vulgar as directly to order Sir Edward Kirby to persuade Fiona to elope with him and to thereby trick her into losing her virginity, but such was implied with many nods and becks and wreathed smiles by the good daughters of faro, and it was left to Lady Disher to take him aside at the end of the evening and name a sum of money that made his boyish blue eyes twinkle like sapphires.

Sir Edward was prepared to meet with heavy competition, but fate played into his hands. Lord Harrington had decided to take himself off to his estates. There was a boundary dispute to settle and repairs to the tenants' cottages to be seen to, discussion of new farming techniques with his estates manager, and a myriad of other jobs to be done, which were more than enough to persuade him to leave town.

The fact was that that cautious misogynist had decided to keep away from Fiona Sinclair until such time as he received news of the respectability or lack of it of her background. All his pet theories about bloodlines and care in marriage were at risk. He felt Fiona had bewitched him. She was like a sickness in his blood, and it enraged him that he should be so held in thrall by a mere girl.

So Lord Harrington, the one person who might have stepped in to warn Fiona before she fell under Sir Edward's spell, was off the scene, and the other, his friend, Mr Toby Masters, had gone with him.

The second ace the fates dealt Sir Edward was that the maid at Number 67 Clarges Street, Alice, caught measles, the latest scourge of London, which was almost more dreaded than cholera. Suitors, learning of the plague at Number 67, kept away, contenting themselves by sending poems and bouquets. Sir Edward had had measles and was therefore in no danger, but he did not mean to tell Fiona that.

The other ace handed to him was Sir Andrew Strathkeith. Mr Sinclair, feeling that nothing could be done to push Fiona out of the nest while there was measles in the house, had found consolation in carousing with Sir Andrew from sunup to sundown. He had also come to the conclusion that Fiona was able to take care of herself, especially when he opened his strongbox and found even more money had been added to it. He conveniently forgot to remind her he had forbidden any more gambling.

Made selfish by strong liquor and a return to his old hedonistic ways, Mr Sinclair left Fiona to nurse the maid. That she should do so personally when she could have easily had hired a nurse did not strike Mr Sinclair as strange. He had known of many Scottish ladies who had devotedly nursed their servants, Scottish households being more democratic than English establishments.

So everything stood fair for Sir Edward.

Perhaps the only other person who felt that there was some good coming out of Alice's illness was Joseph. Although in his heart of hearts, he enjoyed the easy democracy of the hard times in the servant's hall, he was a great stickler for appearances *outside*. The Running Footman was the social centre of Joseph's world and, finicky and over-sensitive, he felt that Luke's courtship of a housemaid diminished him, and therefore diminished his friend, Joseph, in the eyes of the upper servants who frequented the pub.

So when Luke gave Joseph posies of flowers and notes to take to Alice in the sick room, Joseph gave them to Jenny instead, fighting down his guilt by telling himself that he was preventing Luke from social ridicule. Jenny blushed as she accepted the flowers and notes, assuming the fickle footman had transferred his affections from Alice to herself.

He dreaded Luke finding out the trick he had played, but Joseph felt that Luke would thank him one day.

In an age when it was believed that jaundice was cured by swallowing nine live lice every morning, and that a frog tied to the neck stopped nosebleeds, it was as well for Alice that Fiona had met several of the great Scottish doctors of the time who had not been too high in the instep to do charitable work at the orphanage when there was an epidemic – which there frequently was.

Many doctors, such as Abernethy – who had told

an overindulgent alderman to cure his problems by going home and learning to live on sixpence a day, and earning it – had come to believe in the efficacy of a good diet. MacGregor, wooed by Fiona's soft voice and courteous ways, had become her devoted slave and brewed all the herbal potions she suggested without a murmur. Fresh fruit and vegetables began to appear regularly on the servants' table, and Rainbird had instructions to dose them all with a spoonful of cod liver oil every day.

Little Lizzie, standing on tiptoe one morning to peer into the greenish glass above the fireplace in the servants' hall, saw with a kind of wonder that her spots had disappeared. Fresh air was important, insisted Miss Sinclair. Mr Rainbird was instructed to take his small staff walking in the parks as soon as their duties were over.

Weak and listless, Alice nonetheless seemed to be over the worst of her fever and disfigurement by the time Sir Edward Kirby arrived on the scene. Fiona, who did not know Lord Harrington was out of town, had bitterly assumed him to be as afraid of the infection as all the rest.

Normally she would not have received any gentleman with Mr Sinclair gone from the house, but she was so grateful to Sir Edward for his kindness and courage that she entertained him for a whole half hour. It was hard to tell his age because of his cherubic, youthful appearance, but he had travelled a great deal and was able to tell Fiona many strange tales of his journeys in the Ottoman Empire.

He called again the following day. He was merry, he was amusing, and he seemed very harmless. Fiona began to forget about Lord Harrington.

And Rainbird began to worry.

Although he made sure that the door to the parlour was always left open during Sir Edward's visits and that either Joseph or himself was stationed outside in the hall, Rainbird felt he was not doing enough to protect Miss Fiona. He decided it was time to go to The Running Footman, that centre of gossip, and find out more.

Joseph did not notice him coming in. He was happily engaged in talking to Luke. Luke, Rainbird noticed idly, had a face like a fiddle. He heard his name and saw the stately Blenkinsop at the other end of the tap.

After exchanging courtesies, both men got down to the serious upper servants' business of gossiping about their betters. Lady Charteris, who often bragged about the discretion and loyalty of her servants, would have been appalled to hear her affair with a certain Mr Johnson so freely aired.

Both men were drinking shrub. Rainbird ordered and paid for another couple of tankards, and said casually, 'Sir Edward Kirby has been a recent visitor.'

'Ah, well, he would, wouldn't he,' said Blenkinsop ponderously. 'Stands to reason.'

'Why?'

''Cos he likes them young and virginal,' said Blenkinsop. 'They call him The Debutantes' Ruin.

Wonderful how he does it. There was that Miss Pallister who was the reigning beauty back in 1805. He had her. Terrible scandal it was. He left the country, and Mr Pallister had to double the dowry to get her wed.'

'Disgraceful!' said Rainbird, appalled.

'Well, he's a bit of a Don Joon,' said Blenkinsop tolerantly. ''S all right for the gentlemen to be wild. Now, when a *lady* stoops to folly, that's another matter, and, believe me, I do not think I can go on working for her ladyship. A man of my respectability must need look elsewhere, Mr Rainbird.'

'They don't seem to work you hard,' pointed out Rainbird, although his mind was working furiously. 'Both you and Luke are in here a lot.'

'They're often away, that's why. They're staying over in Kensington tonight,' said Mr Blenkinsop. 'At Mr Johnson's.' He drooped one fat eyelid. 'My lord Charteris hasn't any idea of what's going on under his nose. Mind you, they haven't shared the same bed for ten years.'

There was a crash behind them as Luke leapt to his feet and overturned his chair. 'It can't be true,' he said fiercely. 'I won't believe it.'

The tall footman stamped out. Rainbird called Joseph over. 'What have you been saying?' he asked.

'Luke's had a bit too much to drink,' muttered Joseph, with a cautious eye on Mr Blenkinsop. 'I told him Featherbed would win at Newmarket but he would have it that Prime 'Un would come in first.'

Rainbird did not believe Joseph for a minute, but he was too worried about Fiona and Sir Edward Kirby to do other than resolve to get to the bottom of Luke's distress another time.

Rainbird demanded an audience with Miss Sinclair as soon as he got back. He told her of Sir Edward's vile reputation.

'Thank you for your concern, Mr Rainbird,' said Fiona. 'But I prefer to make my own decisions as to the character of my friends. Sir Edward is the only person in London who has scorned the fear of infection to see me.' Rainbird would have protested, but she held up her hand. 'No, Mr Rainbird. And no more plots to secure the heart of Lord Harrington. I never want to see him again.'

But Rainbird did not believe her. It struck him that if he told Lord Harrington of Sir Edward's courtship then the earl might feel obliged to rush to the rescue. With luck, he might be jealous.

He accordingly set out for Hanover Square through the hot, dusty, smelly streets. The heat of the day had been wicked. It was rumoured that Napoleon had hired magicians to cause England to toast like a biscuit.

The streets were not well scavenged, and there were only sewers in the main thoroughfares. A watering cart went past, chased by a swarm of half-naked ragged children. The water poured from a perforated wooden box hung below the axle tree of the cart.

Rainbird began to dream of a post in the country

– some mansion surrounded by cool green trees far from the smells of London with its defective drainage and festering graveyards. Disease lurked everywhere. Miss Fiona had insisted that all drinking water be boiled. MacGregor had tried to protest until Miss Fiona had drawn the cook a neat diagram she had copied from one of the newspapers, which showed that the drinking-water pumps in London houses were perilously close to the cesspools.

An unusual woman, Miss Fiona, thought Rainbird. She should have been an aristocrat with plenty of money so that her brains and modern ideas would not be considered strange. An aristocrat was a pioneer of new ideas: a commoner was stark raving mad.

Rainbird knocked on the door of Lord Harrington's town house. He was hoping for a chat with a friendly butler, but the fat, disapproving face that faced him through a crack in the door changed his mind.

'Miss Sinclair's butler,' said Rainbird in his most pompous tones, 'has a letter of hand to deliver to Lord Harrington.'

'His lordship is at Harrington Court,' said the butler. 'In Kent,' he added gloomily, as if wishing the estate further. 'I will take the note.'

'I must deliver it personally,' said Rainbird, backing away, because he did not have any such note.

'Please yerself,' said the fat butler suddenly and venomously, and slammed the door.

Rainbird made his way slowly back to Clarges Street. The servants' hall was hot and suffocating. Mrs Middleton was drooping over a piece of sewing.

'Come for a walk with me, Mrs Middleton,' said Rainbird.

Lizzie looked up wistfully. She had enjoyed the walks in the parks, but that day Rainbird had shown no sign of taking the servants out.

'I'm sorry, Lizzie,' said Rainbird. 'Go and sit on the steps if your work is done, and get a bit of air. What I have to say to Mrs Middleton is private.'

Mrs Middleton was in high excitement as she stepped out on Mr Rainbird's arm. She hoped passersby would take them for a married couple. Tremulous hope began to rise in her spinster breast as Rainbird led her into the cool shade of the trees in Green Park and said he was looking for a 'quiet spot.' 'God give me the courage not to repulse his advances,' prayed Mrs Middleton.

When they were seated on a bench, at first she could not quite take in what Rainbird was saying because sharp disappointment made her deaf to everything other than the fact that the butler was not making any sort of advances or proposals whatsoever. She gave a resigned little sigh. Mrs Middleton was thirty-nine with a face like an anxious rabbit. She had taken the title of 'Mrs' as soon as she had entered service. She had asked Rainbird to repeat what he had said and at last she was able to grasp he was worried about Miss Fiona and Sir Edward.

Mrs Middleton soon forgot about her spinsterish state as she learned of Sir Edward's wicked reputation. The fact that Rainbird was asking for advice gave her a comfortable glow.

'Mr Sinclair is deaf and blind to anything these days,' said Rainbird. 'My shoulders are aching with the strain of carrying him upstairs to bed o' nights. He hasn't drawn a sober breath since he met that Sir Andrew Strathkeith.'

'But Lord Harrington ... has Miss Fiona confided her feelings to you?'

Rainbird shook his head. That scene in Piccadilly where Fiona had revealed her true background would never be told to anyone. 'All Miss Fiona said,' he replied, sighing, 'is that she is no longer interested in the earl. What her feelings are towards Sir Edward, she has not told me. But her eyes light up when she sees him. Lord Harrington is down on his estates in Kent, so it's not as if he can even be made jealous.'

'Then we will write to him,' said Mrs Middleton firmly.

'Servants don't go writing to earls,' pointed out Rainbird.

'We'll send an anonymous letter by the mail coach,' said Mrs Middleton. 'If he has a spark of feeling towards Miss Fiona, then that should bring him running back.'

But a day before the anonymous letter arrived, Lord Harrington received a long letter from the

Edinburgh lawyers, who pointed out dryly that it had been remarkably easy to find out all about the Sinclairs, Edinburgh still being a small town compared to London, and everyone in it making it their business to know about everyone else.

It was all there. Fiona was a nameless baby left on the steps of St Giles, taken into the orphanage where she had later been employed as a drudge, adopted by Mr Jamie Sinclair, that late great philanthropist who had made it his business to give said orphan his name and all the benefits of a genteel education, although he had adopted the girl as his ward rather than as his daughter. Said Fiona left to one, Mr Roderick Sinclair, brother to Mr Jamie, a retired lawyer, a profligate, low on funds, and hard on drinking.

Mr Roderick had sold up and left for the south with Fiona Sinclair, saying he was going to put her on the Marriage Market. Lord Harrington's lips curled in distaste. What a pair of adventurers they were, the one as bad as the other. And yet he could not think of Fiona as other than the virginal girl she was puffed off to be. Clever and cunning she might be, but he was experienced enough to recognize and remember the innocence behind the warmth and passion.

He was grateful to the lawyers, he told himself, for exorcising the obsession that was Fiona Sinclair. If he had found out such details about her past and they were obviously so easy to find, then others would do the same.

Although he did not want her for himself – for how could he now? – he did not, on the other hand, want to stand back and perhaps see her reputation ruined, leaving her no choice but to join the ranks of the demi-monde.

After some thought, he wrote to his lawyers and suggested they spend as much as they liked to blot out Miss Sinclair's questionable birth. They were to bribe anyone necessary to establish that Fiona Sinclair had been a relative of Mr Jamie and Mr Roderick and that her birth was everything that was respectable. A heavy donation to the orphanage should do the trick. It had been a long-lost relative Mr Jamie had taken from the orphanage, not some nameless bastard. After he had sent off these instructions, he felt free of Fiona Sinclair.

The weather was incredibly hot, and he was drawing up plans to convey water from the lakes on the estate to the surrounding fields. It was absorbing work, and he returned to it gratefully. London, the Season, and Fiona Sinclair faded away.

The next day, he returned from his labours accompanied by his estates manager. Both men were muddied and tired. The earl rang for wine and then settled down to study plans of channels and pipes and ditches.

When the manager had left, the earl was about to go and change out of his working clothes when his eye fell on the morning post, which he had not yet opened. He hesitated. Toby would be back soon from a fishing expedition – although how he hoped to catch anything in this weather was a mystery – and it would be pleasant to settle down to an evening's conversation unmarred by any further land or business worries.

The long windows were all open to let in as much air as possible. Flies hummed over the gallipots in the corners of the room. The cesspool would need to be drained. This was not the weather to put off such a task.

One of the letters caught his eye. It was sealed with a plain blob of red wax and his name was neatly printed on it in capital letters. He sat down and opened it. He read, *Miss Fiona Sinclair is in danger of being ruined by Sir Edward Kirby. A Well Wisher.*

He did not care, he told himself savagely. She and her protector were both swindlers. She had probably written the letter herself.

Lizzie sat demurely on the narrow area steps and turned her little snub nose up to the evening air. After a while, she felt she was being watched, and looked up. Luke, Lord and Lady Charteris's footman from next door, was staring down at her. She blushed and looked down. Such a grand personage as Luke would not want to be seen talking to a mere scullery maid.

'Hey, you,' said Luke.

'Yes, Mr Luke,' said Lizzie, standing up and bobbing a curtsy.

'Come here a minute.'

Lizzie went up the steps and stood shyly at the top.
'Where's Joseph?'

'Cleaning the silver,' said Lizzie. 'He come in five minutes ago.'

'How is Alice?' asked Luke, seeming to choke out the words.

'She is better, Mr Luke, and nigh recovered, thanks to our Miss Fiona, who has nursed her night and day. Jenny is in good spirits, too.'

'Why do you say that? Has Jenny been sick as well? She's the chambermaid, ain't she?'

Anxious to please this magnificent young man, Lizzie said boldly, 'Jenny was ever so pleased with the flowers you sent.'

A slow tide of red mounted up Luke's neck. 'I sent those flowers to Alice,' he grated.

Lizzie looked at him in horror. Luke reached out, caught her thin arm, and twisted it painfully behind her back. 'Has Alice been with a man?'

'No,' whispered Lizzie, blushing. 'How could she? Mr Rainbird is ever so strict about callers. He don't mind you . . .'

Luke gave her a shake. 'Joseph told me in The Running Footman she lay with Palmer.'

Lizzie looked up at him in mute misery.

'Answer me,' said Luke, giving her arm a vicious wrench. 'Did she?'

'N-no,' sobbed Lizzie. 'Alice hates Mr Palmer, same as the rest o' us.'

'Tell Joseph I want to see him,' said Luke. '*Now.* Or I'll throw you down the steps.'

Crying, Lizzie stumbled down the stairs and into the kitchen, where Joseph was polishing the silver.

'What's up with you, Blubber Face?' asked Joseph.

'Mr Luke w-wants t-to see you right away,' gulped Lizzie.

Joseph threw down the pot of rouge and the cloth with which he had been burnishing the teapot. 'Why didn't you say so right away?' he demanded. He took off his baize apron and put on his coat.

'Please don't go, Mr Joseph,' begged Lizzie. 'He's found out . . .'

But Joseph was already out the door and running up the stairs.

MacGregor and Dave listened with interest to the shouts and yells and thuds and blows that were coming from the street above.

'Just two footmen fighting.' MacGregor laughed. 'Nothing to it, Lizzie. Don't distress yourself.'

But Lizzie sat and cried, holding her frail body with her thin arms.

Then there was silence.

Lizzie stood up as dragging steps could be heard coming down the kitchen stairs. Joseph crept into the kitchen. His coat was torn, his nose was pouring with blood, and his lip was cut. He slumped into a chair and for once made no protest as Lizzie cried and fussed over him, bathing his face and trying to comfort him by pointing out that his new livery was due to be delivered the following day.

Rainbird and Mrs Middleton came in and

instantly demanded to know what was up with Joseph. With a pleading look at Lizzie, Joseph explained that he and Luke had had a falling out.

Rainbird looked at the huge purple bruise that was beginning to show on Lizzie's thin arm. 'Where did you get that?' he snapped.

'Mr Luke,' whispered Lizzie, now too overset to do anything other than tell the truth. 'He twisted my arm.'

'Come back, MacGregor,' said Rainbird to the cook, who was about to charge out of the door. 'I will handle this.' Rainbird made his stately exit.

Never had the servants of Clarges Street, who often took the air of an evening when their masters and mistresses were at balls or parties, had such free entertainment. The fight between Luke and Joseph had not been much fun because Joseph had not put up any fight at all.

But *Rainbird* and Luke – that was another matter.

Alice was helped to the window of the attic bedroom by Jenny to watch the fight. MacGregor, with Dave on his shoulders, stood on the area steps. Bets were laid. Rainbird and Luke each stripped to the waist. It took Rainbird a mere ten minutes to lay Luke out on the cobbles with a punishing left.

Downstairs, Joseph, having drained a bumper of brandy, was feeling less ill physically, but mentally he was tortured with shame and guilt. Again, he had had too much to drink at The Running Footman and the lie about Alice and Palmer had come tripping off his tongue. Only when Luke had started to his feet and rushed out did Joseph realize the enormity of what he had done.

'Is telling lies very sinful, Lizzie?' he asked, his eyes round and anxious.

'Oh, yes, Mr Joseph,' said Lizzie seriously, 'but very human, Mr Joseph. We can't be saints, least of all me.'

Joseph gave her a grateful, doglike look, and Lizzie picked up his empty brandy glass and filled it again.

News spread like wildfire that Number 67 Clarges Street was free from infection. But callers found the beautiful Miss Sinclair often gone from home. Fiona enjoyed driving in the park with Sir Edward Kirby. Various gentlemen now went out of their way to drop a hint in Fiona's ear that Sir Edward was bad company for a respectable female, but Fiona had become accustomed to the malicious gossip of London society and preferred to make up her own mind. It was ridiculous to brand someone so innocent and cherubic as Sir Edward a woman-izer, thought Fiona, not knowing that many other females had fallen from the straight and narrow by coming to that same conclusion. He never seemed to want to press his attentions on her. He did not want to talk about politics or the state of the nation, but, on the other hand, he had a fund of amusing stories and a passion for all the latest novels. Above all, he made Fiona feel as if she belonged in this alien world.

Now that she was free to accept invitations, it was pleasant to know that Sir Edward would be there to dance with her and hold her fan and fetch her refreshments. Although Mr Sinclair dutifully accompanied her, his friend, Sir Andrew Strathkeith, always came as well, and the two elderly gentlemen disappeared to drink or play cards as soon as they arrived at whatever function they had escorted Fiona to.

It was surely a guarantee of Sir Edward's good character that he was invited to so many *ton* parties, thought Fiona, not knowing that a rotten womanizer is still socially acceptable, but a lady who falls from grace just once, and is Found Out, is beyond the pale.

Mr Sinclair had taken a strong liking to Sir Edward because Sir Edward always deferred to him in the most flattering way possible.

One of Fiona's first engagements was a splendid ball being held by Lord and Lady Charteris, who had taken their friend Mr Johnson's house in Kensington for the affair because the Kensington house had a large garden capable of housing a marquee for dancing. It was pleasant for the guests to travel the mile from Hyde Park corner to the greenery of Kensington, where the nursery gardens, which grew fruit and vegetables for Covent Garden market, lay spread out on either side of the large white mansions and villas of the rich.

Fiona, as she prepared for the ball, remembered again her impassioned scene with Lord Harrington and thought of it as the mad act of a green young girl. She felt infinitely older and wiser. She was not interested in any man other than Sir Edward, and, although he did not make her pulses beat any faster, at least, with him, she could feel her own woman. Something, however, made her maintain her defensive act of appearing vague and stupid, even with Sir Edward. Perhaps she had been alarmed by Mr Sinclair's statement that clever women only gave gentlemen a disgust of them.

As she was driven along the Brompton Road on the way to the ball in Sir Andrew Strathkeith's lumbering and antiquated carriage with Mr Sinclair and Sir Andrew, Fiona gazed out at the lime trees that lined the narrow way, looking forward to the evening with pleasant anticipation. She had given up gambling – or rather, gambling had given up her, the hostesses of the gambling hells having closed their doors to her – but she had amassed enough to make sure that she and Mr Sinclair could live in a very comfortable style, and even, should she fail to marry, manage very well if they returned to Scotland. Security was added by Sir Andrew's generous offer to give both of them a home.

For the first time in her life, Fiona began to know what it was like to feel young and carefree.

She was wearing a new ball gown she had fashioned for herself out of white-and-blue muslin. It was cut in the Grecian style, with key embroidery at the hem, high-waisted, and with small puffed sleeves. The price of the India muslin had made

Fiona blink, but now she was glad she had bought it for it was cool and light and floated about her body when she moved. Her black hair was dressed in her favourite Grecian style, bound with blue silk ribbons wound twice round her head and with a knot of curls at the back.

She walked into the marquee on Mr Sinclair's arm, oblivious now to the stares of admiration, looking only for the reassuring presence of Sir Edward Kirby.

That was when she saw the Earl of Harrington. Her breathing quickened, and a delicate blush rose to her cheeks.

His topaz eyes fastened on her and then moved to Mr Sinclair. A slow, amused smile appeared on Lord Harrington's face. He walked forward and made a magnificent bow in front of them. 'Mr Sinclair,' he said, 'and ... er ... your lovely ... daughter. How goes it?'

He knows, thought Fiona. He knows, and he is not shocked. Worse than that. He is merely amused and contemptuous.

He chatted to Mr Sinclair and Fiona for a few moments. Dimly she heard herself promising to dance with him. He bowed again and moved away. Fiona searched desperately for Sir Edward, but he was nowhere to be seen. Automatically, she accepted invitations to dance while her mind was a jumble of incoherent thoughts . . . he knows . . . I am sure he knows . . . he is going to bait me . . . oh, where is Sir Edward? . . . please God let him appear . . .

Then the dreaded moment arrived when it was Lord Harrington's turn to lead her through the steps of a country dance. 'You look hot and distressed,' he said. 'Would you care to take a walk in the gardens instead of dancing?'

Fiona said yes and then immediately wished she had not.

Once they were outside, he led her away a little from the noise of the fiddles and said, 'I received a most odd letter when I was in the country.'

'In the country?' said Fiona quickly. 'I did not know you were gone from town.'

'But you should have known! Do not tell me you failed to notice my absence?'

'No. Y-yes,' stammered Fiona. 'That is, I was nursing our maid, who had the measles, so I did not go out and nobody came to call for fear of catching the infection ... except Sir Edward Kirby.' Her voice warmed as she spoke Sir Edward's name.

'Ah, that is what I want to talk to you about. The letter I received was anonymous, but the writer seemed most alarmed that you had been seen in the company of Sir Edward.'

'Sir Edward is all that is good and kind.'

'Sir Edward is one of the most experienced womanizers London has ever known.'

'I am tired of malicious gossip,' said Fiona. 'I am surprised you stoop to it.'

'He will not marry you,' said the earl bluntly.

'There is a better chance of his proposing to me than of *your* proposing to me,' said Fiona dryly.

'Granted.'

'Because,' went on Fiona, moving a little in front of him, her dress fluttering across the lawn, 'you will never marry for love, only for name and rank.'

'Perhaps,' he said, and then, longing to punish her, 'but I would never marry a liar or an adventuress.'

Fiona's face was a pale disk in the twilight. 'Take me back to the ballroom, my lord,' she said in a thin voice. 'Your company fatigues me.'

He felt suffocating anger rise up in him. All the old craving for her, all the old torment, had come flooding back, only this time it was worse than it had ever been. He wanted to crush her in his arms and beg her to marry him, but a wall of pride, as high as a mountain, stood between them.

'As you wish.' He shrugged, but she had already gone before him, her dress giving a last mocking flutter as she disappeared into the marquee and joined the other dancers.

NINE

Friendship is a disinterested commerce between equals. Love,
an abject intercourse between tyrants and slaves.

OLIVER GOLDSMITH

When Sir Edward Kirby appeared, Fiona nearly
disgraced herself by flying into his arms. But she
forced herself to wait until he approached her. She
had kept two dances free, hoping he would arrive.

'You are looking distressed,' said Sir Edward.
'Have you time from all your suitors to walk a little
in the gardens with me?'

Fiona assented gladly, although she shivered,
feeling that the fates were against her and that Sir
Edward would jeer at her and tell her he knew
about her low birth. But he was the same as ever,
pointing out flowers, talking about gardening, until
she was able to feel calmer. How old was he?
wondered Fiona. He was rumoured to be in his
thirties, but he often appeared as young as she
herself.

'Now you are feeling better,' he said, giving her

a sidelong smile. 'Why do you not tell me what ails you?'

'Nothing ails me,' said Fiona. 'The Season fatigues me. All this husband-hunting is wearisome.'

'My beautiful widgeon' – he laughed – 'you do not need to hunt for a husband. All you need to do is crook your finger. Have any proposed?'

'Oh, yes,' said Fiona dully. 'At least five.'

'And you have accepted one of them?' His voice was sharp, and his face in the dim light looked older and almost cunning.

'No.' Fiona sighed. 'Fortunately Papa is too engrossed in his friendship with Sir Andrew Strathkeith to press me to make up my mind. Although he *has* actually said I must not feel I have to marry.'

'A splendid parent ... and a generous one to judge from the splendour of your gowns.'

'I make them myself,' said Fiona. 'Papa is quite as mean as he is reputed to be, I can assure you. What are your views on marriage, Sir Edward?'

'As to that,' he said, plucking a lilac blossom and crushing it between his fingers, 'I fear I am a born romantic. It is not marriage I dread so much as all the tedium of the wedding arrangements, all the questioning relatives, all the marriage settlements. One day, I hope someone as beautiful and good as yourself will simply say, "Let's run away. Let's go to Gretna." It would be monstrous fun, I think – to leave everyone and everything behind.'

Fiona's heart began to beat hard. An elopement

was surely the answer to her problems. No suspicious relative to step in before the marriage, no sharp and questioning lawyer. But what would his reaction be if he ever found out the secret of her birth?

'But you would not run away with a servant or someone of that ilk?' said Fiona.

'Of course not.' He laughed. 'Base-born birth will out no matter how finely dressed up it may appear. I remember a merchant's daughter who . . . Never mind. I will not sully your pretty ears with such a tale. Why should you know of such people? You who are the beautiful daughter of one of Scotland's most famous judges. Let me tell you about the play I saw the other night. Kean was magnificent . . .'

And yet, as he talked, Sir Edward kept darting sidelong looks at her to see if she had taken the bait. It had always worked in the past and was his favourite ploy. Get them to elope, ravish 'em on the Great North Road, return to London unwed, and swear blind and on your oath you were somewhere else at the time and the girl was lying. Lady Disher and Mr Pardon would supply all sorts of useful alibis. Amazing how even the most genteel girls were weighted down with the horrors of family pressure during a Season. Allied to that was the virginal fear of sex. Sir Edward promised escape and boyish, brotherly companionship. And this was what had lured so many young misses to their ruin.

But would he be able to leave such a pearl as Fiona? He had never seen such beauty before. The miser of a father was drinking himself to death. But Sir Edward was genuinely afraid of marriage. Like most womanizers, he affected to like women, and yet he despised and hated them all.

And while Fiona appeared to listen to *him*, her mind was wrestling with the problem of whether Lord Harrington knew her background or not.

Who had told Sir Edward that Mr Sinclair was a judge? Probably Mr Sinclair himself, who had become carried away with what he described as the gullibility of society. Although Sir Edward had said he would not marry anyone base-born, Fiona was sure he would not mind provided he found out the truth only after they were married. But if he should find out before? She realized with a shock she was actually considering marrying him. The idea of an elopement had done it. To run away with someone cheerful and kind, far, far away from London with its perils of gossip.

But if Lord Harrington knew then she would need to risk telling Sir Edward the truth before he proposed. Somewhere in the earl's house he might have papers or a letter. Oh, to be sure!

Fiona allowed Sir Edward to lead her back to the ballroom. Another partner came up to claim her. As Fiona was dancing close to where Lord Harrington was standing with Mr Toby Masters, she heard him say, 'What a dull affair. Let's finish the night at White's.'

Fiona now knew that gentlemen who went to White's Club in St James's Street often did not return home until the dawn, such was the gambling fever that gripped society.

A plan began to form inside her head.

Rainbird yawned as he carried the candle snuffer downstairs. He had been extinguishing the lights after having hefted Mr Sinclair into bed and after having been assured by Miss Fiona that they had no further need of his services until the following day. 'Except it *is* the following day,' grumbled Rainbird. 'It's two in the morning.'

Lizzie was fast asleep on her pallet on the scullery floor. Dave was snoring under the kitchen table. Rainbird picked up his bed candle and began to climb up the stairs from the kitchen and then up the main staircase to his room in the attics. He was just about to open his door when he heard a soft footfall on the stairs below. He blew out his candle and crept back down again as silently as a cat. He could make out the dim shape of Miss Fiona as she stole silently from her bedchamber.

He followed her down the stairs. One oil lamp was left burning in the hall. She was wearing the old cloak in which she had first arrived, its hood hiding her face. She quietly unlocked the street door and let herself out.

Rainbird decided to follow her. The streets could be dangerous at nights, even in the West End. His heart sank as he trailed her into Hanover Square. If Miss Fiona had an assignation with Lord Harrington, there wasn't much he could do to stop it. The earl was a powerful aristocrat and would punish any servant who had the temerity to spoil his pleasure. Keeping under the shadow of the trees in the little garden in the centre of the square, Rainbird watched Fiona.

She went straight up the front steps, which were lit by a huge oil lamp hanging from an iron bracket. She fumbled in her reticule. He heard the chink of money. She walked back down the steps, carefully laying a trail of guineas. She went up and knocked loudly on the door, and then flattened herself against the wall at the side of the door where the rays of the lamp would not shine on her.

There was a long silence.

Then the door opened and Lord Harrington's fat butler appeared, struggling into his jacket. He peered about, cursed, and was about to close the door, when he saw the gold. From his viewpoint, Rainbird could see the gleam of avarice in the butler's eyes. The butler bent down, picked up the first gold piece, and then moved down the shallow steps, picking up the rest. The shadow that was Fiona detached itself from the wall of the house and silently glided inside.

The butler searched and searched until he was sure he had all the gold. Then he went inside, shut the door, and locked it.

What is she up to? wondered Rainbird. What can I do? Glad he was still wearing his old black velvet livery instead of his splendid new suit, he sat down under the trees and prepared to wait. If there was a scream or yell from the house, then he would be on hand to run to the rescue.

Fiona had remembered seeing a large desk in the library where Lord Harrington had entertained her. She waited a long time in the darkest corner of the hall after she had heard the butler lock up and retire.

The house was very quiet and still. The smell of sugar and vinegar from the gallipots made the warm air cloying and close. Finally Fiona moved again, feeling her way in the blackness of the hall towards where she knew the library to be. With infinite slowness and care, she gently opened the door.

She had taken the precaution of bringing a tinderbox with her and also a stub of wax candle. She started the laborious process of lighting the candle. She took off the lid of the flat round brass tinderbox and struck a piece of agate against a piece of steel. Any spark that fell on the tinder, which was of cotton rag, had to be blown and carefully tended until it became a red glow. Then a thin splint of wood, the end tipped with sulphur, was held over this incandescent bit of cotton, and, if you were lucky, it lit the first time. Fiona was not lucky, and it was a full twenty minutes before she was able to light the candle.

To her relief, she was in the right room. The candlelight flickered on the tortured face of the mangled deer. She crossed to the desk and carefully went through all the drawers. There were account books, business documents, and blueprints, but no personal letters at all.

Made bold by desperation, she decided they must be abovestairs in his dressing room or bedchamber. She opened the library door and listened carefully for several moments. No sound at all.

She decided to keep the candle lit rather than risk colliding with someone in the dark. If she did meet some servant, she would need to pretend to be one of Lord Harrington's doxies, and hope to escape because of the embarrassment *that* would cause. Her usual commonsense, which might have told her that Lord Harrington would hardly entertain doxies, if he had any, in his own home, had deserted her. But the servants were obviously all abed and Lord Harrington would surely not be home until the dawn.

The first floor boasted a drawing room, a saloon, and various small reception rooms. The bedrooms were obviously on the second floor. It was easy to tell which was Lord Harrington's since it was the only one in use. His nightshirt was laid out on the bed and jewels spilled from the jewel box onto the toilet table.

She saw an escritoire in the corner of the bedroom and gently lifted the lid. Various letters were stuffed in pigeon-holes. Although they were personal letters, none related to her. In her worry and frantic haste, she began to be convinced he had documents concerning her and that he had hidden them somewhere. Her eyes fell on his jewel box. It was a large box of the kind with trays that lifted out. Jewels spilled about her as she lifted the top tray out – stickpins, diamond buttons, sapphire buckles, ruby and emerald rings.

She stooped to pick them up.

The door opened, and Lord Harrington stood on the threshold. There was a footman behind him, holding a branch of candles. The house was so thickly carpeted that Fiona had not been warned of their approach.

The earl looked at Fiona, kneeling in the circle of candlelight, her hands full of jewels. His face went hard and set. He turned to the footman, his large figure screening Fiona from the servant's view. 'Go away, Paul,' he said, 'and inform the other servants I am not to be disturbed, no matter what you hear.'

He waited until the footman had left. Then he stepped into the room, locked the door, and put the key in his breeches pocket.

Outside in the square, Rainbird sat biting his nails. Lord Harrington's arrival home had come as a shock. So Fiona did not have an assignation. She had crept into his house for some other reason. At first he had thought that the ruse with the gold had been so that Lord Harrington's servants would not see her. Now Rainbird felt certain she had stolen quietly into the house like a thief to find something ... or take something. Was she a thief? Uneasily Rainbird remembered her generous gifts of money, money she said she had come by gambling. Lord

Harrington had stood on the step for ages chatting to his friend, Mr Masters. He had not looked like a man who knew that a beautiful lady was awaiting him indoors.

On the other hand, worried Rainbird, taking another chew at his nails, perhaps Miss Fiona was trying that old trick of compromising the gentleman. He had seen the light of her candle in the upper room and had assumed she had gone into his lordship's bedroom. Yet Rainbird knew in his heart that Fiona was pure and virginal. So she must be a thief. And if she were caught, the disgrace would be terrible.

A scream rent the air – a scream suddenly stifled.

Rainbird jumped to his feet and began to run. There must be some way into the house round the back.

Fiona crouched motionless on the floor. Her hood had fallen back. Her cloak was loosened and showed she was still wearing her ballgown. Her eyes were great black pools.

Lord Harrington shrugged off his coat, wrenched off his cravat, and proceeded to undo the buttons of his shirt.

'What are you doing?' asked Fiona through white lips.

'Getting ready to bed you,' he said, his calm, even voice more frightening than if he had screamed or yelled. He took his shirt off, crumpled it into a ball, and threw it in a corner. 'You do not want to appear in court and neither do I. You will pay for the jewels you have stolen with your body.'

'I have stolen nothing ... *nothing!*' said Fiona, rising to her feet.

'Then why are you here?'

'I came ...' faltered Fiona. 'I came ...'

He shrugged, walked forward, and hooked his hand into the bosom of her dress, jerking her against him. Fiona looked up into his eyes. They were blazing with fury and hate.

'No!' she screamed. 'Oh, *no!*'

His mouth came down on hers, cutting off her scream of protest. His mouth was punishing and savage, his tongue, thrusting between her lips, probing and searching. The hand holding the bosom of her gown jerked downward. There was a rending sound and then Fiona felt her bare breasts crushed against his naked chest. The fact that she was still wearing her cloak open over her gown made her, paradoxically, feel doubly naked.

She wriggled to free herself, but the movement of her breasts was so erotic that he became deaf and blind to everything but the passion submerging him. With one Herculean effort, Fiona wrenched her mouth free.

'I came to find the papers,' she cried. 'Only the papers. I could not find them anywhere and thought they might be under your jewels. In pity's name, *hear me!*'

'What papers?' he demanded.

'You know about me,' whispered Fiona. 'You

know. I saw it in your face tonight. But I had to be *sure.* You could ruin me.'

Then there was a knock at the door, a loud, imperative knock. The earl frowned. His servants would not disobey his orders. 'Who is it?' he called

'Rainbird, my lord,' came a loud voice. 'Miss Sinclair's butler come to take Miss Sinclair home.'

'The deuce,' said the earl savagely. He thrust Fiona away from him, feeling sick and ashamed. 'Cover yourself,' he snapped. Fiona drew the folds of her cloak tightly about her.

Lord Harrington pulled on his shirt again and stuffed the tails into his breeches. Then he unlocked the door. 'How did you get in?' he demanded.

Rainbird bowed. 'You left the front door open, my lord. I thought I heard Miss Sinclair scream.'

Lord Harrington swung round and looked at Fiona, his eyes blazing. 'You and your accomplice may leave,' he said. 'I have no wish to bring scandal to my good name by taking you both to court.'

Rainbird stepped quickly round him and picked up the candle. 'Come, Miss Fiona,' he said gently. 'It is late.'

With bowed head, Fiona walked forward, past Rainbird, past Lord Harrington, to the door. Rainbird followed her with the candle.

Lord Harrington went after them to the landing and then leaned over, watching them both descending the stairs. Fiona suddenly stopped and looked up. 'I brought that disgraceful scene on myself, my lord,' she said, her voice sad and gentle. 'Do not reproach yourself. And Rainbird here, he knew nothing of it. He must have followed me through concern for my welfare. Ah, you, my lord, with your lands and title, will never know what it is to be poor and nameless.' She pulled her hood up about her head and continued on her way down.

Lord Harrington stayed where he was, stunned and shaken by conflicting emotions, watching the light glimmering and bobbing as she and Rainbird made their way downstairs. He heard the key turn in the street door. So he had not left it open. Rainbird must have found another way in. He turned and walked back to his room, opened the window, and leaned out so that he could watch her crossing the square.

'Miss Fiona,' Rainbird was saying urgently. 'You look so white. Please tell me what happened.'

'I cannot, Mr Rainbird,' said Fiona. 'I never want to think of it or remember it again.'

'Your face is set and hard. You are become old,' fretted Rainbird, studying her face in the pale grey light of approaching dawn. 'Smile for Rainbird.'

Their voices carried clear up to the earl as he stood at the window of his bedchamber.

'Did I ever tell you, Miss Fiona,' coaxed Rainbird, 'that I used to perform at fairs when I was a boy? How merry I was! And how I made them laugh. I would play the mandolin, like Joseph, and I would dance.' He performed a mad, capering dance and then turned several cartwheels, doubling back to land neatly upright in front of Fiona. 'Smile, Miss Fiona.'

'Oh, Mr Rainbird,' said Fiona, beginning to tremble. 'I am lost.' She threw herself into his arms and sobbed as if her heart would break.

Rainbird put an arm about her shoulders, and talking nonsense, coaxing and pleading, he led her out of the square.

The earl watched them until the two figures were swallowed up in the dark shadow cast by the black bulk of St George's Church. Then the square swam in front of him, and he found his eyes were full of tears. He knew now she had spoken the truth, knew it in the very marrow of his bones. She had merely been looking for evidence that he had found out all about her.

To the devil with his lands and his title and his pride, he thought, striking his fist into his palm. He would call on Sinclair in the morning and beg for Fiona's hand in marriage. He would *make* her marry him. No other woman would do.

But he had nearly raped her. Would he really have gone so far? He had frightened her and abused her. The words she had said to him on the stair tormented him.

He lay awake for a long time, tossing and turning, wondering at what time of day that old toper, Sinclair, would awake. At last he fell into an uneasy sleep and dreamed that he was trying to catch Fiona, who was always just in front of him among a colourful, shifting fairground crowd. Every time he nearly came up to her, she would dance away from him with Rainbird doing cartwheels at her side.

TEN

❧

It ain't the 'unting as 'urts 'un, it's the 'ammer, 'ammer,
'ammer along the 'ard 'igh road.

PUNCH

❧

'Why so fine, why so haggard, and why so early?'
asked Mr Toby Masters.

'I am going courting, Toby my friend.' The earl
grinned. 'In fact, congratulate me, although I fear
that may be premature. I am going to beg Miss
Sinclair to marry me. For that matter, what are you
doing about so early yourself? It is only nine o'clock
in the morning.'

'As to that, it was about Miss Sinclair that I came
to see you.'

'Never say you are going to try for her yourself!'

'No. Look, it's like this.' Mr Master's fat face was
creased with worry. 'I couldn't sleep. The heat was
suffocating, so I decided to go for a ride in the park.
I was coming back along Piccadilly about sevenish
when a closed carriage went past me travelling at a
great rate. Up on the box, muffled up to the ears

186

despite the heat – that was why I noticed him – was Sir Edward Kirby.'

The earl's heart began to hammer against his ribs. 'And . . . ?'

'And although the carriage blinds were down, as it drew abreast one of the blinds sprang up and there was Miss Fiona Sinclair.'

The earl sat down suddenly on a chair in the hall. Toby had come upon him just as he was leaving.

'You see,' said Mr Masters awkwardly, 'it came across me at that ball that you were head over heels in love with the girl. I thought she had perhaps a tendre for you. But,' burst out Mr Masters, turning red, 'there's that damn pride of yours. I began to think only a dowager duchess would be considered good enough for you. When I saw Miss Sinclair . . . she looked so pale and *hurt.*'

'If I don't get her back, if I don't stop her,' said the earl grimly, 'I will never forgive myself.' He jumped to his feet and shouted for his fastest racing curricle to be brought round. 'I know they've gone to Gretna,' he cried. 'Or at least I'm sure that's where Sir Edward has told Miss Sinclair they are going.'

'I will come with you,' said Mr Masters.

'No, Toby. Go instead to Clarges Street and tell that butler, Rainbird, what you have seen. I swear neither her servants nor her . . . father know of this.'

Mr Masters hurried out and swung himself up on his horse with surprising ease, considering his bulk.

Rainbird heard him coming. It was unusual to

hear someone riding hell for leather in the streets of the West End where none of the top ten thousand poked his nose out of doors until the afternoon. He did not know that, after he had seen the sobbing Fiona to her room, she had not slept, that she had waited until he had fallen into an exhausted sleep, and that she had crept from the house, carrying only one small trunk, and had made her way to Sir Edward Kirby's lodgings in Jermyn Street.

Mr Masters was breathless and sweating. Words came tumbling out of his mouth one after the other and Rainbird had to plead with him to take it slowly. When Rainbird grasped that Mr Masters was saying that Fiona had eloped with Sir Edward, his shock was almost as great as the earl's. He remembered how he had eventually managed to prise the whole story out of Fiona of what had happened in the Earl of Harrington's house on that sad road home at dawn.

Rainbird had shaken his head dismally over the whole thing. It was quite clear to him that Miss Fiona was in love with the earl, but that the earl, like all the aristocrats that Rainbird had known, would never marry a girl with a doubtful background and would certainly never marry any young miss who had the temerity to break into his house in the small hours of the morning.

What if the earl had not known of Fiona's background? What if there *was* no evidence? Then the earl would merely think her a common thief. To be found with your hands full of jewels and then say you had only been looking for papers – particularly if the earl did not have any such papers – looked very bad.

When he grasped from the heaving, sweating Mr Masters that the Earl of Harrington had been on his way to Clarges Street to beg Mr Sinclair to allow him to pay his addresses to Fiona, Rainbird's heart gave a lurch. Fiona was somewhere on the Great North Road and everything that might have made her life happy had come too late.

'We'll catch 'em,' said Rainbird. 'Lord Harrington may miss them if Kirby goes off the main road. All of us will go and if . . . if Kirby's done anything he should not, then he'll be forced to take her to the nearest church and marry her.'

'I-I d-do not have a carriage,' stammered Mr Masters, backing before the fury in Rainbird's eyes, although that fury was not directed to him.

'We'll hire one,' said Rainbird. 'I have money. We'll get the best.'

Old Mr Sinclair snored upstairs in a drunken sleep as Number 67 Clarges Street roared into life. Soon servants from the adjoining houses turned out to watch the goings-on at Number 67.

First a big, fat gentleman – Mr Masters – arrived with a spanking open racing carriage, drawn by four matched bays. To the watchers' surprise, all the servants from Number 67 began to pile in. 'I'm not very good with a four-in-hand,' panted Mr Masters, 'and these tits are fresh.'

'I am,' said Rainbird curtly. He took the reins. Mr

Masters sat beside him. In the back were Mrs Middleton, Alice, Jenny, Lizzie, and MacGregor – who was clutching a large blunderbuss. On the back strap stood Joseph and Dave.

'Hold tight!' called Rainbird. 'I'm going to spring 'em.'

The watching servants sent up a ragged cheer as Mr Masters and the entire staff of Number 67 raced round the corner into Piccadilly. Mrs Middleton clutched her bonnet and let out a faint scream. Elated beyond words, Dave produced a yard of tin and blew a deafening blast.

'Don't go charging through the turnpikes,' shouted Mr Masters, holding on to his hat with one hand and the side of the box with his other. 'We'll need to keep asking if anyone has seen them.'

Mr Percival Pardon crackled open the stiff parchment of a letter that had been brought into him with his morning chocolate.

It was from Sir Edward Kirby, he noticed from the seal. When was the man ever going to get on with it? Bessie Plumtree had discovered that a certain Mr Benham, who she was sure was smitten by her charms to the point of marriage, had up and proposed to Fiona Sinclair and had been turned down and now stated his intention of taking his broken heart out of the country. She had turned up at Mr Pardon's the night before with her parents and had blamed him for doing nothing to stop Fiona from wrecking the hearts of all the eligible young men in London. Lady Disher, the sobbing Bessie had said, had promised them all that Mr Pardon would arrange things. Then Lady Disher had called on Mr Pardon, told him he was an idiot, and said that Sir Edward Kirby seemed to be falling in love with Fiona just like every other fool.

Mr Pardon scanned the note, and then a pleased smile crossed his face. He took off his chin strap the better to enjoy the pleasure of rereading the words. Success! That very morning, Sir Edward had written, Fiona Sinclair had called at his lodgings and *begged* him to elope with her. He would be back in town in a few days' time to collect his reward before leaving for the Continent.

Mr Pardon sipped his chocolate contentedly. He would give an impromptu party in two days' time. It would amuse him to invite all those who had been at that first dinner party at his home on the night of the storm, all those who were in London, that is. He would also invite Lady Disher and the gambling hostesses. He would wait until they were all gathered and then have the delight of telling them that he, Percival Pardon, had risen to Machiavellian heights. Fiona Sinclair was no longer a threat!

Rainbird wished he had brought more money. Each time they changed the horses, the price was more expensive because they demanded only the best from each posting house. It seemed odd that prices should rise the further one went away from

London, but such seemed to be the case. He felt he had taken a considerable sum, but it seemed to be dwindling fast.

The light was turning to that greenish violet colour of twilight as the burning sun slowly slid down the sky to bury itself behind the parched fields.

Was there ever such heat! The trees, which would normally have been clothed in the delicate green foliage of spring, were dusty and heavy with their summer leaves. Roses as large as cabbages hung over the hedges of cottage gardens, appearing well before their time. Lines of smoke rose up into the suffocating air from fires at the side of the road set off by sparks from the wheels of the heavy traffic on the Great North Road.

They were all weary and tired. But at each turnpike, they learned they were hot on the trail and not only had Sir Edward Kirby been spotted but also Lord Harrington – 'looking like the devil hisself' – had gone through ahead of them.

Sir Edward, who had hoped to disguise his appearance by muffling up, had on the contrary caused people to notice him who might not otherwise have done so. Only a mad-man would wear a muffler in this weather.

Lizzie sat silently praying for Fiona's safe-keeping. She was covered in dust. Her pretty new gown was dirty. It was actually of the cheapest cotton, but it had a little design of rosebuds round the hem. Mrs Middleton had sniffed and had said it was too saucy-looking for a scullery maid, but Rainbird had not only insisted that she have it, but had given her two more gowns as well.

Lizzie had been much comforted to learn that Lord Harrington was looking for Fiona. She had never seen him, but felt reassured by the thought that someone so high in rank would surely be a match for the likes of Sir Edward. But something else was making her feel uneasy. She had a feeling there was something they had not done that they should have done. The carriage lurched and swayed over the sun-baked ruts as Lizzie desperately tried to remember what it was.

Jonas Palmer had arrived back in London the day before after a pleasant journey to various of his master's establishments where he had been fawned on and entertained by the servants.

Palmer would not admit to himself that there was something about Rainbird that frightened him. And so he told himself on the following day that there would be no harm in a visit to The Running Footman just to pick up a bit of casual gossip about what was going on at Number 67.

The tap was quiet when he pushed open the door. There were only a few servants. A pompous old man in butler's livery was sitting at a table. With a great effort of memory, Palmer identified him at length as that butler, Blenkinsop. Adopting a bluff and hearty manner he accosted Blenkinsop and asked him what he would like to drink.

Blenkinsop was only too delighted to have a fresh audience to listen to the sinful iniquities of his mistress, Lady Charteris. Palmer patiently heard him out, and then asked idly, 'I hear my tenant is a bit of a miser.'

'Oh, Mr Sinclair,' said Blenkinsop. 'Yes, that's the tale. But you can't say the same for the beautiful Miss Sinclair. Spoils those servants rotten. Gives them money and new livery, and they've all gone out driving in the finest turnout you've ever seen.'

Palmer's eyes widened. 'I might step around and see what is going on. All gone driving, you say? The deuce! I have forgotten my keys.'

'They went off and left all the doors open,' said Mr Blenkinsop. 'Anyone could walk in.'

'Indeed? I'll see to that.'

Palmer made his way out and along to Clarges Street. As Blenkinsop had said, the street door was standing open. Leaning over the area railings, Palmer noticed the kitchen door was open as well. He walked in the front door and called loudly.

No reply.

Above him in his bedchamber Mr Sinclair slept on.

'She gave them money, did she?' mused Palmer. 'Wonder where Rainbird's hidden it. Isn't good for servants to have money. They might get frisky and think o' leaving.'

He went down to the servants' hall and searched diligently about, going through everything from the butler's pantry to the scullery and the kitchen, even ripping open Lizzie's bed to see if the money had been hidden there. Then he remembered Mrs Middleton's little parlour.

He went up to the half landing on the kitchen stairs and pushed open the door. It was a tiny room but as neat and sparkling as a new pin. Palmer heard a groan from far above his head and a masculine curse.

Mr Sinclair! Of course! Blenkinsop had said nothing about either Miss Sinclair or the old man having been in the carriage with the servants. He ripped things apart and turned things upside down on the floor in his haste.

Then there it was, in front of him all the time. A japanned box on the window ledge. He jerked it open. It was full to the brim with sovereigns and notes. A small fortune. Whistling between his broken teeth, Palmer tucked the box under his arm and made his way swiftly out.

By george! He'd give a monkey to see that Rainbird's face when the butler came back and found his means of escape gone.

Fiona slept for most of the day, and Sir Edward did not bother to awaken her at any of the posting houses when he changed horses. He wanted to get her as far away from London as possible in case she woke up and changed her mind.

He did not plan to take her to any out-of-the-way inn. He had done things like that early in his womanizing career, but had found that small innkeepers were apt to turn puritan while the landlords of very expensive posting houses could be easily bribed to turn a blind eye. Fiona had assured him she had left no letters and had told no one what she planned to do or where she was going. He did not anticipate any pursuit.

He would lie with her that night. If she were willing, so much the better. If not, he would drug her. Either way, Fiona Sinclair would see the next dawn with her reputation in ruins while he made his way back to London to collect his reward.

He was sweating freely, and, feeling more secure as the distance from London lengthened, he tore off the suffocating muffler. Only a mile to go and then they could rack up for the night. He was tired to death, but he still had work to do. Lady Disher should know how hard he had strived to earn his reward. It was a good thing Fiona Sinclair was such a quiet, placid sort of female. She must still be asleep. She had not raised a murmur.

By this time, Fiona had actually been awake for two hours and had spent the time in first grieving over Lord Harrington and then in beginning to remember all she had heard about Sir Edward Kirby. Things about him began to come back to worry her as well, things she had been too anguished and upset to take in during her flight.

When she had asked him to elope with her, he had not said one word of love. He had readily assented, but, as he had turned away to straighten his cravat in the looking glass, Fiona, who could see his reflection, had noticed an odd gloating look on his face.

He had rented the carriage. The master of the livery stables had brought it around himself and had said something with a snigger about expecting his turnout back in the usual two or three days. Fiona had not paid any particular attention at the time, but now it nagged at her mind.

Her thoughts swung back to Lord Harrington. He was irrevocably lost to her: if there had ever been a chance of securing his affections, then it was gone.

Although he had treated her shamefully, he had thought she had come to rob him. And yet . . . there was no need to make love to her. He could have called the watch, or, as he said he did not want to become embroiled in a scandal, have simply called his servants and had her turned out. Then he had said nothing at all about having known anything of her past.

Back went her thoughts again to Sir Edward. It was surely unusual, even during an elopement, not to have servants. Surely it would have been wise to have outriders and grooms for the long, perilous journey north to Gretna Green on the Scottish borders, where fleeing couples were married in vulgar haste by the blacksmith over his anvil?

Fiona bit her lip. Her long sleep had served to clear her brain. As soon as they stopped for the night, she planned to sit down and write a long letter to Mr Sinclair, telling him not to worry about her because she was going to . . .

She sat up straight. There was one great, huge, immovable obstacle to her marriage to Sir Edward Kirby, Fiona realized with an aching heart. She loved Lord Harrington, and always would, and marriage to another man, however kind, would do nothing to make the sick longing go away. It would have been better simply to have persuaded Mr Sinclair to go back to Edinburgh.

Fiona felt guilty about leaving him. He had been drinking too much and would not live very long unless she were around to try to put a stop to it. She would need to pluck up courage and tell Sir Edward it had all been a mistake.

Fiona longed to change her clothes, which were sticking to her body. She raised the carriage blinds and jerked down the glass, breathing in great gulps of hot scented air.

The carriage began to slow its pace. They lumbered under the arch of a posting inn and rolled to a stop outside the door. Fiona, looking out at the grandeur of the posting house, which was called The Pelican, reflected gloomily that she was putting Sir Edward to a great deal of unnecessary expense.

Sir Edward opened the door and smiled at her. She smiled back, although she thought he looked a shocking mess with sweat channelling rivulets through the dust that coated his face.

'Wait there a little, Miss Sinclair,' he said, 'while I see to the booking of our rooms.'

Fiona sat patiently after he had gone, rehearsing various speeches in her mind. Feeling the confines of the carriage too hot and stuffy, she stepped down into the courtyard of the posting house and looked about her with interest.

Ostlers stood and gawked at her beauty. Coachmen came from the stables and looked in awe. Servants emerged from the inn. Sir Edward appeared with the landlord and cursed under his breath as he saw Fiona standing in the middle of a circle of admirers. He had forgotten the stunning effect of her beauty on all who saw her.

'Put the hood of your cloak over your face,' he snapped as he came hurrying up.

He reminded her so much of Mr Jamie that Fiona looked at him and said, 'No. It is too hot.'

He muttered something rude and hustled her into the inn. They would dine first, he said.

'I am hot and dusty,' said Fiona firmly. 'I must change and bathe.'

'I am sharp set,' he said crossly. 'I have bespoke a private parlour. No one will see us.'

Fiona's eyes, those large grey eyes that usually looked on the world with an air of wide-eyed innocence, turned on Sir Edward. They were as hard as steel. 'I said, I will bathe and change first, and then I have something to say to you, Sir Edward.'

The servants were listening, so he gave in with bad grace.

It was only when the landlord was leading Fiona up to the bedchamber that Sir Edward realized she would find his belongings in it, because he had, as usual, reserved only one bedchamber, there being no point in the expense of two when he meant to seduce the girl. But he marched to the tap for a much needed drink of ale. He would think of some excuse.

The landlord held open the door and ushered Fiona into a large bedchamber on the first floor. Fiona crossed to the open window and looked out. There was a pretty garden at the back, and a pond, the areas of black mud around it showing where the water level had sunk.

'Is everything in order?' came the landlord's voice.

'Yes, thank you,' said Fiona, turning round. 'Wait a bit,' she said sharply. 'Those trunks at the end of the bed are not mine. You have given me the wrong room.'

'Well, they're Sir Edward's trunks,' said the landlord with a worldly smile.

Fiona raised delicate eyebrows. 'Then take them to his room,' she said.

The landlord edged a finger into his shirt collar. It was not only Fiona's great beauty that was so intimidating; it was also the force of her personality, which seemed to fill the room.

'Beg pardon, miss. This *is* his room.'

'Then pray take me to *my* room.'

'Sir Edward bespoke only one room.'

There was a long silence. Fiona's eyes seemed to bore into the landlord's very soul. Then she suddenly said with a charming laugh, 'As usual, of course.'

The landlord's face cleared and he winked, 'Quite so, madam.'

'Tell Sir Edward to meet me in the private parlour in half an hour's time,' said Fiona.

Smirking with relief, the landlord bowed himself out.

Fiona resolutely bathed and changed as if her world had not come roaring about her ears. At last, she was dressed in a muslin gown, only slightly creased from the packing. She brushed her hair and twisted it up in a knot on top of her head, then drew on her gloves.

She picked up the first of Sir Edward's trunks, walked to the open window, and threw it out into the pond. It sank slowly with a satisfactory, gurgling sound. Returning from the window, Fiona collected the two other smaller trunks and threw them out as well. A white duck looked up at her with an almost human look of amazement on its face.

Fiona let out a long breath. She had quickly come to terms with the fact that Sir Edward was a villain. She squared her shoulders and set out for the private parlour.

Sir Edward was still in his travelling clothes. He had passed a wet towel over his face, but that was as much as he had done to make himself present-able. He looked nervously at Fiona as she entered the parlour. She gave him a bewitching smile as she sat down at the table and shook out her napkin.

He gave her a relieved smile. He tried to make conversation about the strain of their hectic drive, but Fiona ate steadily, not even looking up.

At last, after the covers were removed and the servants had left them alone, Sir Edward said, 'Very quiet, ain't we?'

Fiona dabbed her lips with her napkin and threw it down. 'I am now ready to talk to you,' she said, looking up. Her face was hard and set. If she had been Aphrodite at the beginning of the meal, now she was Artemis.

'What about?'

'About your intentions.'

'My intentions? Why, to marry you, my love.'

'Why did you only book one bedchamber?'

'We are to be married, so there is no harm in . . . er . . . getting to know each other better.'

'I am sure you can wait a few days,' said Fiona calmly. 'It is not as if you have evinced any signs of mad passion.'

'As you please,' he said hurriedly. He could feel his boyish mask slipping and hurriedly straightened it. 'What you must think of me!' He laughed. 'The fact is the inn had only one bedchamber left and so–'

'I pushed open a few doors as I came along here,' said Fiona, 'and the bedchambers were empty.'

'That curst landlord!' exclaimed Sir Edward. 'He has lied to me. Of course, guests may be due to arrive later. Hark! Someone is arriving now.'

The sound of a carriage being driven at great speed sounded from the road outside the inn. But whoever it was had evidently decided to stop their mad ride and after a little the vehicle could be heard turning into the courtyard.

Sir Edward thought quickly. He should have drugged the wine. Too late and too difficult. He studied Fiona's neat head. One good blow should suffice. Get it over with and have her on the floor. All he wanted to do was sleep and sleep. 'Go and see who it is,' he said, hoping to catch Fiona off guard.

She went to the window and looked out. But, like the bedchamber, it overlooked the pond at the back of the inn. She turned back – and then jumped to one side with the agility of a cat. The bottle Sir Edward had been going to bring down on her head smashed against the window frame. Drops of red wine stained the muslin of Fiona's gown.

She ran to the door, but he caught her by the shoulder and spun her back. She seized a ripe peach from the bowl on the table and threw it full into his face. As he clawed at the pulp, she ran again for the door, but he dived after her, seizing her legs and bringing her crashing down.

He pinned her to the floor. Stunned and winded, Fiona tried to summon up all her strength to escape as she felt greedy hands fumbling in her gown. The weight of his body was suffocating. Her head hurt. She could not move.

The door opened and jarred against their bodies. Fiona had one glimpse of the Earl of Harrington's tortured and furious face. Sir Edward was plucked from her as if he weighed no more than a child. Both casement windows had been opened to let in the maximum amount of air.

Lord Harrington held Sir Edward by the seat of his breeches and the scruff of his neck. He swung him back and forth several times while Sir Edward fought and kicked helplessly. Then he flung him clean through the window. There was a long descending wail and then an almighty splash.

From the kitchens downstairs the landlord watched Sir Edward fall and wrung his hands. 'Oh, he'll kill me, too,' he moaned, meaning Lord Harrington, before whose stormy arrival and imperious demands he had just fled after telling him where to find Fiona. 'All I can do is swear to my innocence.'

Lord Harrington came back and knelt on the floor beside Fiona and took her in his arms. 'Marry me,' he said huskily.

'I can't,' said Fiona shakily. 'I am a nameless orphan. I do not know the names of my parents. It is doubtful if my mother, whoever she was, was ever married to my father.'

'I know,' he whispered, holding her close. 'I know and it does not matter. I drove you into running away with that lecher, did I not?'

Fiona nodded dumbly.

'Has he touched you? Has he harmed you?'

Fiona shook her head. 'He tried to stun me. I was so silly. I did not think he would resort to violence. I thought I could handle him.'

'Wait here until I deal with him further.'

Fiona wound her arms about his neck. 'You *want* to marry *me*?' she asked dizzily.

'Oh, yes, my heart, my life.'

And Fiona kissed him.

And the Earl of Harrington promptly forgot about Sir Edward and everyone and everything else in the whole wide world as he returned her kiss with savage ferocity, which gradually calmed into dreamy, caressing passion.

Sir Edward struggled frantically from the mud of the pond. He would gain the front of the inn, call for his carriage, and escape from the hellish terror that was the Earl of Harrington. He stumbled around the front of the inn, wiping the mud from his face with his sleeve.

But his nightmare had only just begun.

Into the inn courtyard came an open carriage that was crammed with people who all screamed and pointed at him. He recognized Fiona's butler.

He dived past them, across the road, and into the fields beyond, sobbing his way through the darkness as the whole staff of Number 67 Clarges Street bayed at his heels like hounds.

Upstairs in the private parlour, Lord Harrington had finally left off kissing Fiona to explain how he had learned of her elopement, how he had re-organized her past, how nothing in the world mattered except that she be his wife.

Fiona listened to him, her eyes shining. The earl went on to say he had old friends who lived close by. They would travel there that very evening, and, if his friends were willing, as he was sure they would be, they would be married in their family church.

'I will send my servants back to London to fetch Mr Sinclair,' said the earl. 'When we are married, we will go to my home in Kent. I am weary of London. I never want to see the place again.'

Fiona raised her lips to his, but, before he could kiss her, there came a terrible row from the staircase outside. The earl set her aside and went and opened the door.

Stumbling up the stairs with MacGregor's blunderbuss in his back and with the rest of the servants crowding behind came the sorry figure of Sir Edward Kirby.

'Oh, my lord,' cried Rainbird thankfully. 'I am glad you are here. We caught him as he was escaping. How is Miss Fiona?'

'Well,' said the earl, grinning. 'We are to be married.' He backed into the room as the servants pushed Sir Edward in front of them.

'He is so muddy,' said Lizzie, looking at Sir Edward.

'I had finished with him,' said the earl, smiling down at her. 'I have no more time for him.'

'What did you do with him, my lord?' asked MacGregor.

'I threw him through that window.'

'Oh, weel,' said MacGregor cheerfully, 'seeing as how you don't want him ony mair . . .'

He nodded to Rainbird, and together they threw Sir Edward back through the window and into the pond.

'You are brave and courageous servants,' said the

earl. 'Toby! I did not see you. You shall attend our wedding.'

'And all the servants,' said Fiona. 'They must never go back to work for that awful Palmer again.'

'As to that,' beamed Rainbird, 'I, too, have a surprise. With the money you gave us, I am going to buy a little inn at Highgate village. We will all work together to make a success of it. We will all be one family.'

Lizzie burst into tears of joy as the rest, with the exception of Joseph, cheered. Joseph could not envisage living anywhere else but in the West End of London.

'Maybe Alice won't want to come, Mr Rainbird,' said Mrs Middleton, 'her being so keen on young Luke.'

'I ain't keen no more,' said Alice in her slow, country voice. 'He hurt little Lizzie. Just think what he would do to a wife!'

'Yes,' murmured Miss Fiona Sinclair, looking up at the earl under her lashes. 'Those brutal men are so untrustworthy.'

Two days later, Mr Percival Pardon looked about the room at his guests. They were all so sour, so down in the mouth, that he longed to see their faces lighting up when he made his announcement.

At last, he could wait no longer and held up his hands for silence. 'Listen!' he cried. 'Great news. Fiona Sinclair has fallen mercy to the wiles of Sir Edward Kirby. See, I have his letter. Let me read it to you.'

Bessie Plumtree burst into angry tears and Harriet Giles-Denton stared at him with contempt. Lady Disher walked forward and plucked the letter from Mr Pardon's hands. 'You utter fool,' she said. 'Did you not read your newspaper? It was in the social column this morning. Fiona Sinclair is to wed the Earl of Harrington and rumour has it that Sir Edward has left the country a broken man. We all knew. We thought *you* knew and were trying to make up for your ineptitude by entertaining us. Faith, Pardon, you always were a weak and useless fop!'

And so the Earl of Harrington and Miss Fiona Sinclair were married and all the Clarges Street servants were guests. Only Mr Sinclair was absent, being confined to bed with what was diagnosed as Flying Gout.

Joseph had become reconciled to the idea of being a publican. It had been a wonderfully lazy life for them all the few weeks before Miss Fiona's wedding. Although they were put up in the servants' wing at Lord Harrington's friends' mansion, they were not expected to work.

Joseph, bored at first, had discovered a very sympathetic listener in Lizzie and he often went for long walks with her, bragging of what he meant to do in the future while Lizzie looked up into his face, her eyes like stars.

But even as she stood at last in the church and watched Miss Fiona being married, Lizzie still had that same nagging fear at the back of her mind.

Before she left with her new husband, Fiona sent for Rainbird, looking affectionately at the butler with his acrobat's figure and comedian's face.

'Well, my Rainbird,' she said softly, 'all's well that ends well. Are you sure everything will go smoothly with you now? My lord and I are going to be travelling abroad for some time after we have left Mr Sinclair in Kent, where he can be cared for by a competent physician. I do not wish to leave the country if I feel you still need my help.'

'No, my lady,' said Rainbird. 'Thanks to you, we shall all do very well.'

'Then hug me, Mr Rainbird, as you have done when I was upset and miserable. Hug me, now that I am glad.'

Rainbird opened his arms, and Fiona threw herself into them.

'What is this?' demanded a voice from the doorway. The Earl of Harrington stood surveying the scene, his arms folded.

'I was only saying goodbye to Mr Rainbird,' said Fiona.

The earl looked at Rainbird and jerked his head in dismissal.

'Never let me see you with your arms around another man again,' Rainbird heard the earl say as he went down the stairs. 'Do you want to kill me with jealousy?'

Rainbird began to whistle.

He, Rainbird, had made an earl jealous.

EPILOGUE

The November wind whistled down Clarges Street, a biting bone-chilling wind. It rushed down the area steps of Number 67 and moaned under the kitchen door.

'Faith, 'tis cold,' said Rainbird gloomily. 'What's for supper, MacGregor?'

'Naethin' but bread and cheese,' snapped the cook.

'I kent stend it,' wailed Joseph. 'We're all cold and miserable and hungry again. Next time anyone wants meh help, they can whistle for it.'

'I will never regret helping Miss Fiona,' said Rainbird severely. 'Never.'

'I know Palmer took the money,' said Jenny fiercely. 'Mr Blenkinsop told Mr Rainbird Palmer knew the house had been left open. Besides, Mr Sinclair's money wasn't touched.'

'We can't prove it,' said Rainbird with a pessimistic shrug. 'He was seen going in. He said he discovered the robbery and called the watch, which there is proof he did.'

'It's as if we're taking care of ghosts,' said Alice with a shiver. 'Every day we take down the shutters and clean and scrub the rooms, but there's no one there.'

'I still keep thinking of that dear little inn,' mourned Mrs Middleton, who had been sure Rainbird would propose to her once they had thrown off their servants' shackles, hope springing eternal in the spinster breast.

'Can't yer write to Miss Fiona – I mean 'er ladyship and ask 'er to 'elp?' said Dave.

'We don't know where she is,' said Rainbird. 'I waited too long, thinking Mr Sinclair would have told her all about it, but evidently he did not. He was so ill at the time, he probably thought it all part of a dream.'

'We're all together,' said Lizzie stoutly. 'That's very important. If you love people, it's more important than money.'

Joseph sniffed and looked away. He felt he had paid too much attention to Lizzie while they were in the country and had given her ideas.

'P'raps,' said Alice slowly, 'somewhere there's another tenant, looking at the advertisement. Give us a tune, Joseph. Ain't no use bein' miserable as I can see. Waste o' time.'

Joseph brightened and went to fetch his mandolin.

Lizzie was right, thought Rainbird. They would survive, just so long as they all kept together.

Mr Sinclair climbed stiffly down from the mail coach outside the post office at the west end of the North Bridge in Edinburgh. He was feeling much fitter than he had done for many years.

Fiona had frightened him with a lengthy lecture on the perils of drinking too much. After the happy couple had left for abroad, Mr Sinclair had stayed on at the earl's home in Kent until he had felt strong enough to make the long journey home.

His determination to remain teetotal had been further strengthened by the shocking death of his old friend, Sir Andrew Strathkeith.

He breathed in a great gulp of sharp, sooty Edinburgh air, then left his trunks at the post office and decided to amble forth in search of accommodation.

His steps bore him across the bridge to the towering black tenements of the Old Town. His eyes filled with sentimental tears. The Royal Mile, with its bustle and filth, its dangers of being hit with the contents of refuse pails or chamberpots thrown from above, might make the genteel Londoner shrink, but it was like heaven to the returning Mr Roderick Sinclair.

In front of St Giles Church were the rows of sheds called lucken booths where the traders sold everything imaginable. The air rang with their cries, resounding with Scottish voices.

And then sweet and clear above his head rang out the 'meridian'.

His steps led him to John Dowie's tavern. All good resolutions were forgotten. But he paused with his handle on the door. He suddenly thought the whole episode of going to London had all been a dream. Had he really met the top ten thousand on an equal footing? Had Fiona really existed? Had he really been called the Miser of Mayfair?

Then he heard Fiona's voice inside his head,

saying, 'Do you want to die? Your death is in each bottle. Oh, *it* may not kill you. But what of the insanity of trying to hang yourself?'

'How did ye ken ah was going to hang myself,' said Mr Sinclair sulkily. A passerby looked at him nervously.

Mr Sinclair turned and walked rapidly away from the tavern door, and the further away he walked, the lighter he felt.

There were a good few years left to him.

And, after all, he was home.